the TOTAL PARTY SYSTEM
FAIRY TALE HANDBOOK
by Total Party Skills

Classic Fantasy Characters

The Total Party System
Fairy Tale Handbook
By Total Party Skills

Classic Fantasy Characters
Written by R Joshua Holland
Cover and Interior Art via Public Domain
No A.I. was involved in this composition
Copyright 2024

WARNING: Some Classic Art May Contain Mild Nudity

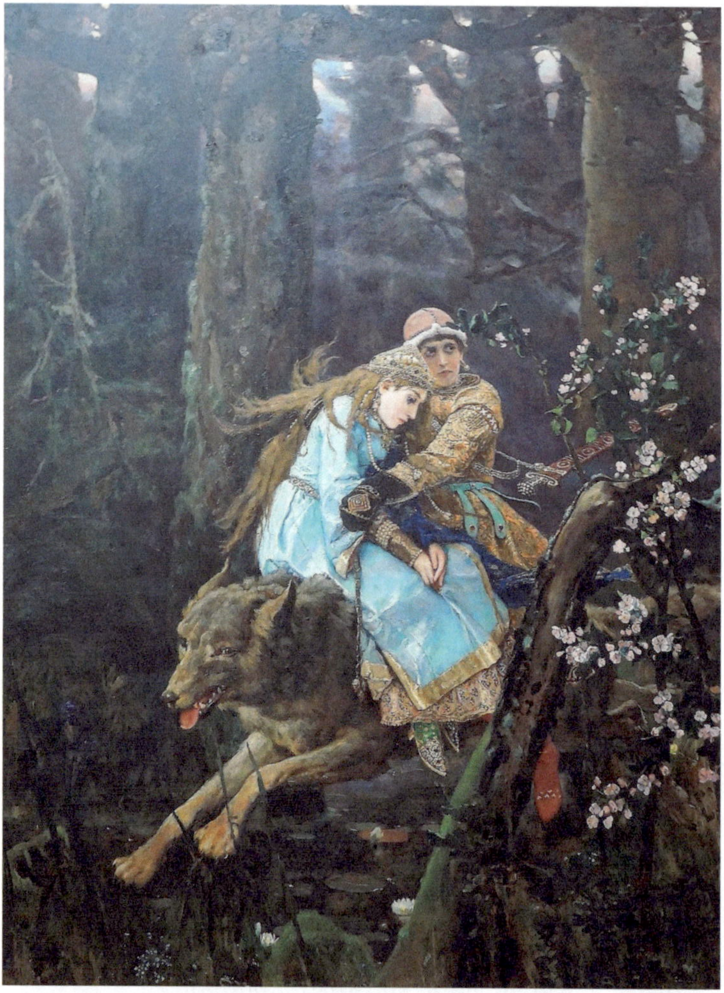

Table of Contents:

Classic Fantasy Characters	p. 7
Peasants & Wenches	p. 12
Lords & Ladies	p. 22
Clergy & Maidens	p. 32
Wizards & Witches	p. 40
Outlaws	p. 52
Fairy Folk	p. 58
Fairy Friends	p. 120
Shapeshifters	p. 170
Fairy Foes	p. 210
Fairy Treasure	p. 278

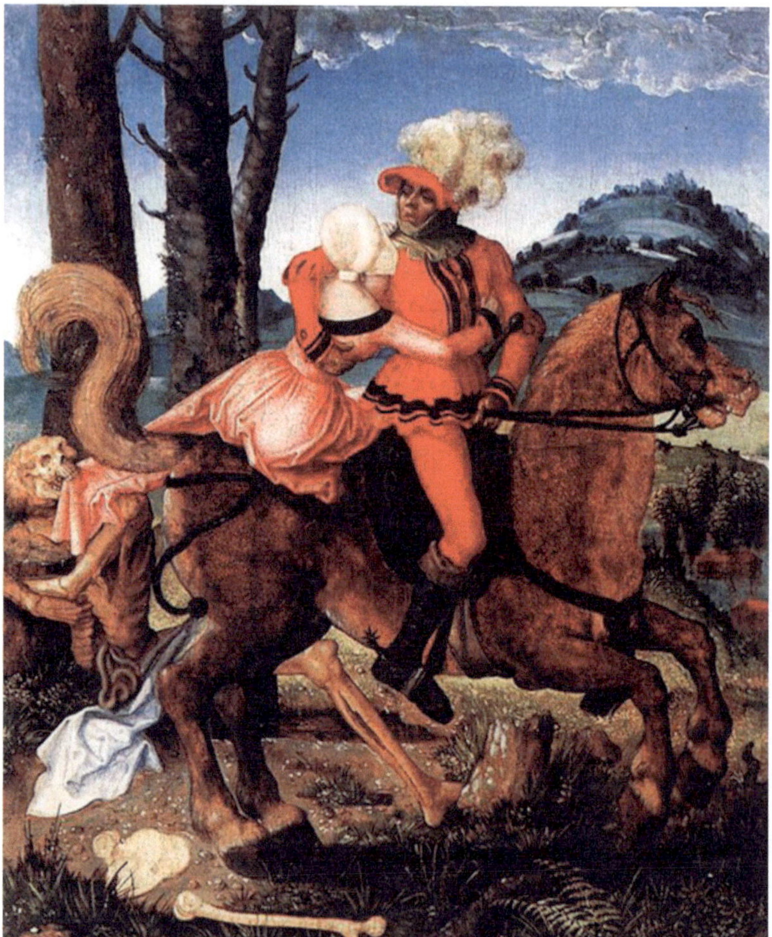

Classic Fantasy Characters

The Total Party System Fairy Tale Handbook presents a wide range of options for Characters in a classically formatted (pre-20th Century) fantasy campaign. The materials within are setting-neutral and designed to work with the Total Party System Rules Handbook. This is not a complete game, merely a resource to build a Fairy Tale style adventure or campaign around, based on the Characters and Creatures available in this book. These options are compatible with other Total Party Skills games, but are not presented with any of the lore attached to those specific settings.

The Fairy Tale Handbook is not intended for children. It draws inspiration from an older and darker presentation of fantasy that predates modern sensibilities, but there are lessons to be learned by Role-Playing through the struggle to overcome the limitations of a much more rigid way of life than we now enjoy. This Handbook is recommended for Adult and Young-Adult players.

All Classic Fantasy Characters created at starting level of experience (Level 0) using this Handbook will have the same range of Attribute Scores, and will determine their Status levels in the same manner. Human characters recover lost Status, and will have the standard Human Limit Values, as described in the Total Party System Rules Handbook. Some Inhumans may have different rules of recovery, special abilities, and Limits as described in their section in this Handbook.

Level-0 Characters start with Attribute Scores of 1. They will then receive 3 points that they may add to their Scores, with no Score permitted to be raised higher than 3. The Attributes are BODY, MIND, and SPIRIT.

They will determine their maximum number of STATUS levels as follows:

HEALTH: Body +2
SANITY: Mind +2
MORALE: Spirit +2

Human Characters have the following LIMITS:

ENCUMBRANCE: 1 + Body + Strength
MOVE/COMBAT: 1 + Body + Agility
MOVE/TRAVEL: 1 + Body + Strength

Once Attributes and Status have been determined, the Player will need to Select a ROLE for their Character. This will determine if they are Human or Inhuman, their Social Class, their Primary School of Skills, and what Item Options are available to them at the start of the game.

HUMANS:

ROLE	CLASS	SKILLS
Peasant	Commoner	Mind
Wench	Commoner	Body
Lord	Nobility	Combat
Lady	Nobility	Strange
Clergyman	Church	Divine
Maiden	Church	Spirit
Wizard	Nobility	Psionics
Witch	Outlaw	Occult
Outlaw	Outlaw	Martial

INHUMANS:

ROLE	CLASS	SKILLS
Elf	Nobility	Psionics
Pixie	Church	Divine
Gnome	Commoner	Strange
Goblin	Outlaw	Occult
Ogre	Commoner	Martial
Satyr	Outlaw	Occult
Mermaid	Nobility	Psionics
Centaur	Commoner	Body
Cherub	Church	Divine
Swan Maiden	Nobility	Martial
Werewolf	Outlaw	Martial
Selkie	Church	Divine or Spirit
Nymph	Nobility	Strange
Pooka	Commoner	Body or Mind
Cat-Sith	Nobility	Psionics or Occult

Each Role will describe their Skill options, the Items they can begin with, and provide some general information about their Social Class. Characters are illiterate unless they have placed points in the Languages Skill.

Inhuman Roles will include additional information on any special abilities, different methods of recovery, and their Limit Values, if they are different than those of a mortal human.

Game Masters should be encouraged to use their discretion and limit the Roles available for their players to choose from, to best suit the needs of their adventure or campaign. Not every Fairy Tale is appropriate for Inhuman Player Characters, and sometimes it's the other way around. Consider your adventure's setting and objectives when deciding which Roles to make available. Players should always check with their Game Master before selecting their Character's Role.

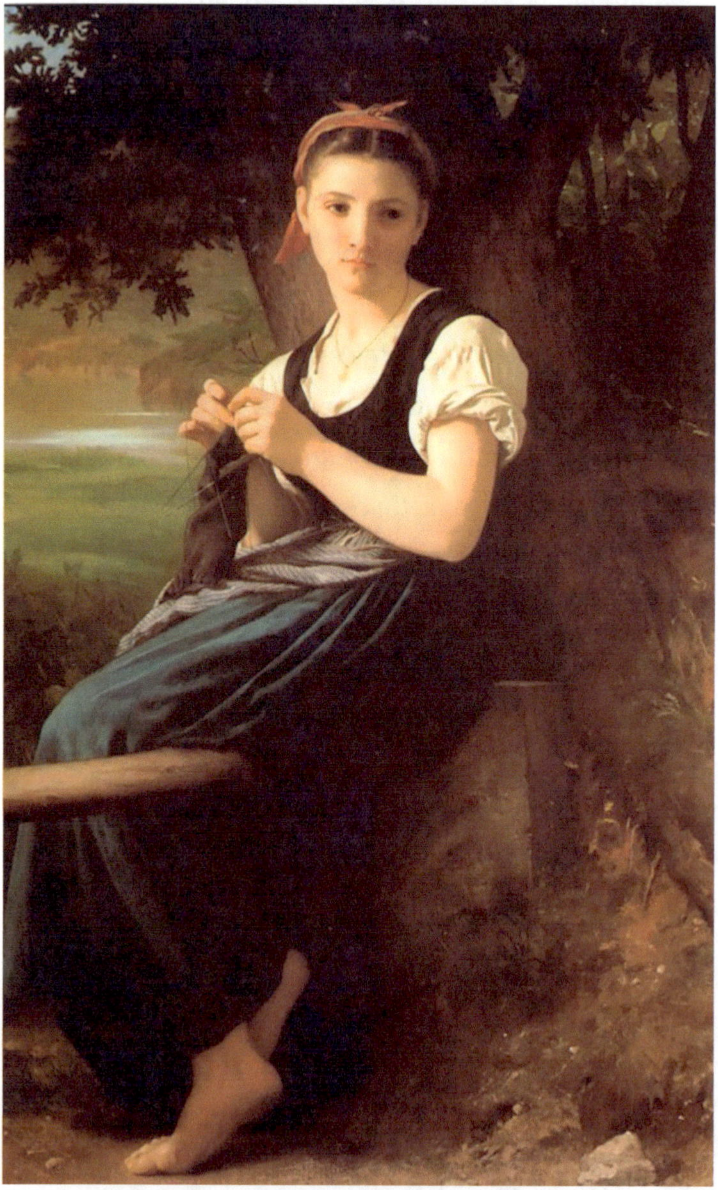

Peasants & Wenches

Peasants and Wenches represent the Common Folk of medieval times, and are frequently caught up in strange business and unexpected adventure in many a classic Fairy Tale. Their Social Class, "Commoners", gives them little access to wealth, property, and influence, but they do enjoy an easier time maintaining their anonymity, and can call on other Commoners, as well as the Church, for aid and shelter.

Peasants and Wenches receive most of their income from their work on a Noble Estate, or by being a (likely highly-taxed) professional in a town or city. They will have a home, possibly shared with family, but they will not own it. They are either expected to work for their right to housing if they live on an estate, castle, or manor, or they will pay rent in more urban environments. Commoners are typically paid, and make transactions with, Copper Coins or Bartering.

Peasants and Wenches receive 5 points to place in skills in their Primary School. For Peasants, this will be the Mind Skills of Knowledge, Perception, and Technology, and for Wenches, Agility, Beauty, and Strength. No Primary Skill may be raised higher than +4 with points at starting level of experience. After Primary Skill points have been spent, the Player will select an Occupation for their Peasant or Wench Character. This will indicate a specific skill that they receive a +1 bonus for. This Bonus is allowed to raise a skill as high as +5 if it is in their Primary Category.

After this Occupational bonus has been applied, the Character then receives 9 points to add to skills in their Primary Category, their Occupation Skill, or to any skill in the Schools of Mind, Body, Spirit, Combat, or Strange. Skills from outside of their Primary School cannot be raised higher than +3 during Character Creation.

Peasants and Wenches are Human and use Human Recovery and Limit Values.

PEASANT:

Peasants are adult humans who are required to work to support their Nobles, their Church, and their Families.

CLASS: Commoner
PRIMARY SKILLS: Mind

OCCUPATION	BONUS	ITEM
Tailor	Agility+1	Sewing Kit
Squire	Beauty+1	Stablehand Kit
Farmer	Strength+1	Donkey or Goat
Steward	Knowledge+1	Noble's Stamp
Shepherd	Perception+1	Staff
Blacksmith	Technology+1	Hammer
Merchant	Charisma+1	Item of Choice
Guard	Focus+1	Padded Armor
Sailor	Boxing+1	Net
Lumberjack	Melee+1	Ax
Archer	Ranged+1	Bow
Carpenter	Art+1	Tool Kit
Traveler	Languages+1	Backpack
Hunter	Strike+1	Dog
Soldier	Parry+1	Sword
Jester	Dodge+1	Funny Hat

STARTING COINS: 10+Body (Copper)

WENCH:

Wenches are adult humans who have to work to support their Nobles, their Church, and their Families.

CLASS: Commoner
PRIMARY SKILLS: Body

OCCUPATION	BONUS	ITEM
Servant	Agility+1	Noble's Stamp
Dancer	Beauty+1	Makeup Kit
Chambermaid	Strength+1	Lamp
Gossiper	Knowledge+1	Cat
Nanny	Perception+1	Flask
Seamstress	Technology+1	Sewing Kit
Barmaid	Charisma+1	Club
Confidant	Empathy+1	Jewelry
Prostitute	Melee+1	Dagger
Weaver	Art+1	Loom (counts as 2 Items)
Translator	Languages+1	Foreign Book
Cook	Science+1	Cooking Kit
Fortune Teller	Clairvoyance+1	Tarot Cards
Virgin	Blessing+1	Jewelry (Holy Symbol)
Pagan	Demonology+1	Incense
Medium	Necromancy+1	Lamp

STARTING COINS: 10+Spirit (Copper)

16

WENCH MAGIC:

Wenches who have skill points in Blessing, Demonology, or Necromancy will know 1 Spell or Blessing at the start of their adventures, from a limited selection of options, as indicated below. They can learn new spells in the manner described in the Rules Handbook, but will require either an instructor or mentor who has a higher bonus in the skill in question than the Character seeking their aid, or they will need access to the proper research materials, (often books), which will require their Character to also be literate. Beginning Spells are Hard to Cast until they can be re-trained.

BLESSINGS
Luck
Guidance
Forgiveness

DEMONOLOGY SPELLS
Spirit Calling (by type)
Ward Against Spirits (by type)
False Appearance

NECROMANCY SPELLS
Shadow Vision
Summon Ghost (by name)
Bind Ghost (by name)

COMMONER EQUIPMENT:

Peasants and Wenches begin the game with either a Peasant Dress or Tunic+Leggings, a set of occupationally appropriate Work Clothes, and a pair of sandals, shoes, or boots. They will receive the Item listed with their chosen Occupation, and may make 2 selections from the following options:

ARMOR	DEFENSE	DETAILS
Winter Coat	Padded	1/2 damage from cold
Leather Cuirass	Padded	
Wool Hat	Padded	
Leather Cap	Padded	
Small Shield		Parry +2 *

Wearing a Coat+Hat or Cuirass+Cap gives wearer Plated Armor Defense.

*A Small Shield requires one free hand to use, and can be slung over the back as a worn Item when not in use (does not count against Encumbrance Limit when not in hand)

WEAPONS	DAMAGE	RANGE
Sling	1	4
Dagger	1	close
Hammer	1	close
Staff	1	1
Spear	2	2
Whip	1 +1 Morale	1
Ax	3	close
Club	2	close
Bow	2	8

EQUIPMENT	DETAILS
Backpack/Sack	+2 Encumbrance
Quiver of Arrows	6 Arrows
Oil Lamp	2 hours between refills
Bottle of Oil	4 Lamp Refills
Fire Kit	start a fire
Tool Kit	+2 repair actions
Sewing Kit	repair cloth, stitch wounds
Camping Kit	Bedroll and
Stablehand Kit	+2 Horse's Beauty for 4 hours
Makeup Kit	+1 Beauty for 4 hours. 12 uses
Jewelry	+1 Beauty
Cooking Kit	Cooking Utensils and Spices
Cooking Pot	Make a Meal
Bundle of Torches	5 Torches, burns 1 hr each
Blanket	Stay warm at night
Canteen/Flask	1 day water ration
Fishing Pole	Catch a Fish: Body+Technology
Pipes	Make Music
Drum	Keep a Beat
Fiddle	Make Music
Rope	50 feet long

LIVESTOCK
Dog
Cat
Donkey
Goat

COMMONER

Name: Level:
Role: Primary Skills:
Occupation: XP:

ATTRIBUTES/STATUS

BODY HEALTH

MIND SANITY

SPIRIT MORALE

SKILLS

BODY
Agility
Beauty
Strength

MIND
Knowledge
Perception
Technology

SPIRIT
Charisma
Empathy
Focus

COMBAT
Boxing
Melee
Ranged

STRANGE
Art
Languages
Science

MARTIAL
Dodge
Parry
Strike

PSIONICS
Clairvoyance
Psychokinesis
Telepathy

DIVINE
Blessing
Exorcism
Healing

OCCULT
Demonology
Metamorphosis
Necromancy

LIMITS
ENCUMBRANCE: DAILY PRAYERS:
MOVE/COMBAT: SPELL MEMORY:
MOVE/TRAVEL:

ITEMS
Armor: Weapon:
Other:
Spell/Blessing:

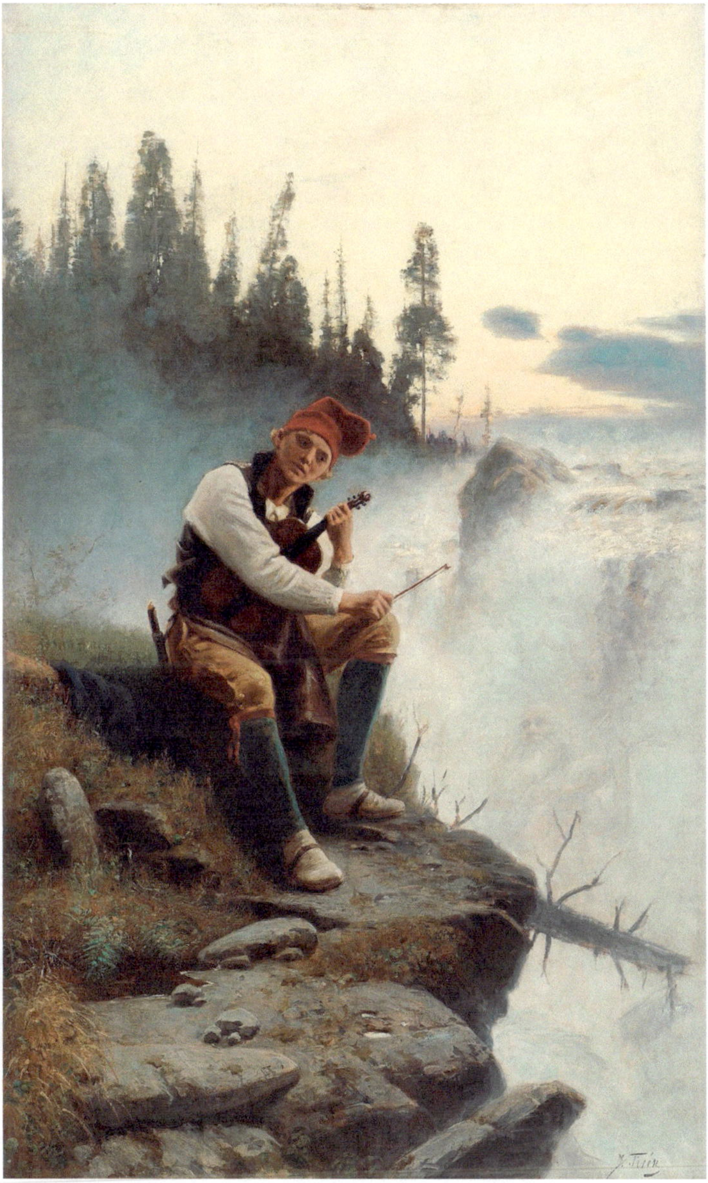

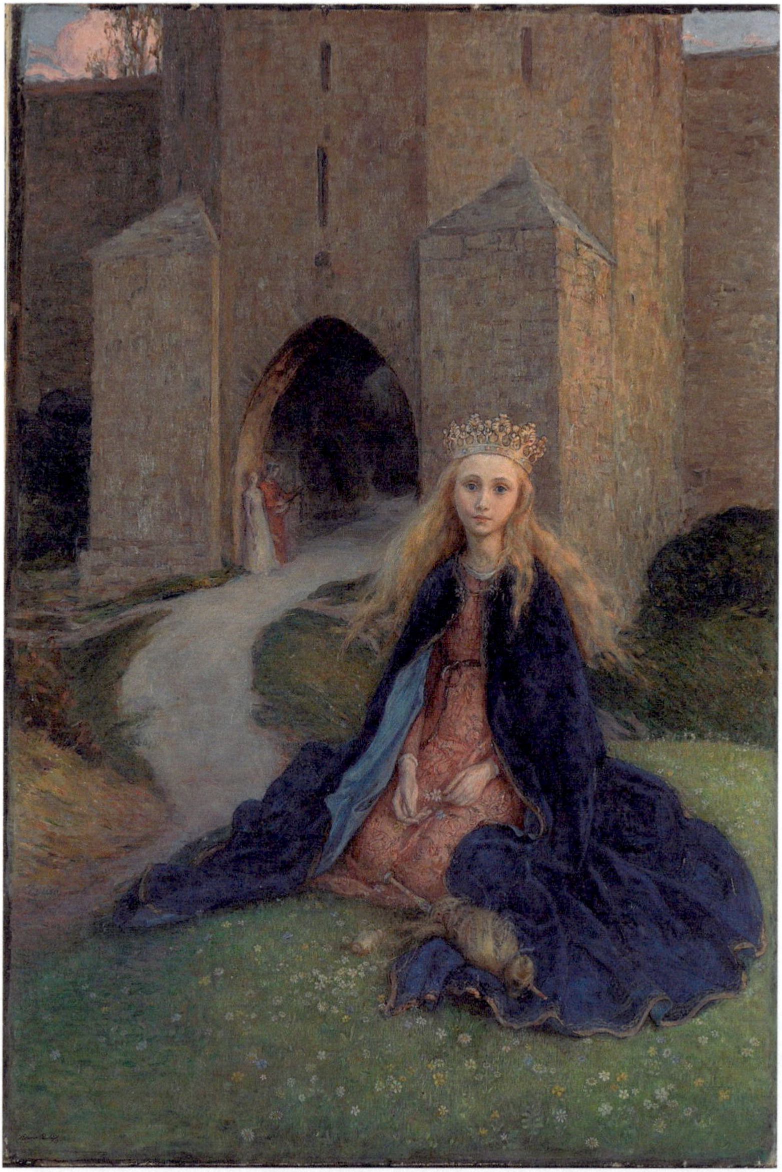

Lords & Ladies

Lords and Ladies represent the ruling Noble class in classic Fairy Tales. They gain their authority from a combination of birthright, military force, political acumen, and the sanction of the Church. A Noble can make do without one of these four things, but the more that are missing, the harder it will be to hang on to their lands and title.

Commoners, Members of the Church, and even Outlaws can join the Nobility by gaining a knighthood from a ruling Noble or Church official, giving them the right to own land and gain the privileges of Noble Title, or by marrying into an established Noble Household. Otherwise the only way to become a Noble is to be born to a Noble parent, or through elaborate scheming. Military command, service to the Church or Kingdom, political or public popularity, or donations of large sums of coin to Church or Noble coffers are the most common ways a Character could gain a Knighthood and earn the rank of Sir or Madame.

Only Nobles are able to become Rulers of their lands, although in times of weak rulership the Church will often step in to fill the void of public service. Nobles are paid and make purchases in Gold Coins. Characters born into the Nobility will have either the Role of Lord, or the Role of Lady. They will receive 5 points to spend on skills in the Primary School associated with their Role. No Primary skill may be raised higher than +4 with points at starting level of experience.

The Player will then select their Character's Title, followed by their Character's Archetype. Each will indicate a skill that the Character receives a +1 bonus to, and can potentially raise a Primary Skill to +5. After their Title and Archetype bonuses have been applied, the Character will then receive a final 8 points to add to skills in their Primary School, their Title and Archetype skills, or skills in the Schools of Body, Mind, Spirit, Combat, and Strange. No skill outside of their Primary categories may be raised higher than +3. The choice for a Character's Title will also list an Item that *the Character owns at the beginning of their adventuring.*

TITLE	BONUS	ITEM
Sir	Melee+1	Sword
Madame	Languages+1	Tea Service Kit
Baron	Charisma+1	Large Shield
Baroness	Agility+1	Jewelry
Count	Knowledge+1	Crossbow
Countess	Focus+1	Makeup Kit
Duke	Perception+1	Knight Armor
Duchess	Empathy+1	Bottle of Poison
Prince	Technology+1	Squire + Jewelry
Princess	Beauty+1	Handmaiden + Jewelry

ARCHETYPE	BONUS
Athletic	Strength+1
Tough	Boxing+1
Precise	Ranged+1
Talented	Art+1
Educated	Science+1
Ruthless	Strike+1
Witty	Parry+1
Nimble	Dodge+1
Visionary	Clairvoyance+1
Faithful	Blessing
Inspired	Healing
Corrupt	Demonology

LORD

The heir or ruler of a Noble Estate, duty bound to their superiors, and to their King or Queen.

CLASS: Nobility
PRIMARY SKILLS: Combat

TITLE	STARTING COINS
Sir	10 + Melee (Gold)
Baron	15 + Charisma (Gold)
Count	Mind x10 (Gold)
Duke	Spirit x20 (Gold)
Prince	Body x50 (Gold)

Lord Characters begin the game with a set of Fine Clothes and boots, the Item listed with their chosen Title, lodging in an estate, castle, or manor that they either own or will inherit, and a Horse. Plus 2 additional Items of Choice from either the Commoner Equipment options, or from the Noble Equipment options at the end of this section.

LADY

A potential heir or ruler of a Noble Estate, duty bound to their superiors, and to their King or Queen.

CLASS: Nobility
PRIMARY SKILLS: Strange

TITLE	STARTING COINS
Madame	10 + Focus (Gold)
Baroness	15 + Knowledge (Gold)
Countess	Spirit x10 (Gold)
Duchess	Body x20 (Gold)
Princess	Mind x50 (Gold)

Lady Characters begin the game with a Nice Gown and shoes, the Items listed with their chosen Title, lodging in an estate that they either own or will inherit, and a Horse (possibly intelligent). Plus 2 additional Items of Choice from either the Commoner or Noble Equipment options.

NOBLE MAGIC:

Nobles who have points placed in the skills of Blessing and Demonology have had little time to train their abilities between the responsibilities of ruling territory. Nobles skilled with Blessing will know a number of Blessings for Items equal to their Spirit Score, selected from those listed in the Rules Handbook.

Nobles skilled in the Occult will know 1 spell for each point placed in the Demonology skill, selected from the following options. Starting spells are Very Hard to cast until they can be re-trained.

DEMONOLOGY SPELLS
Spirit Calling (by name)
Spirit Summoning (by name)
Ward Against Spirits (by type)
Astral Travel
Simple Apparition
False Appearance

Characters skilled in Demonology can craft new spells as described in the Rules Handbook.

NOBLE EQUIPMENT:

ARMOR	DEFENSE	DETAILS
Chainmail	Plated	
Knight Plate	Full Suit	
Large Shield		Dodge+2 Parry+2
Horse Armor	Plated	for the horse

WEAPON	DAMAGE	RANGE
Sword	2	close
Crossbow	2	4
Health Poison	5	
Lance	4 with mounted charge attack	1

EQUIPMENT	DETAILS
Bottle of Poison	5 doses
Belt of Bolts	12 Bolts for Crossbow
Tea Service Kit	Make and Serve Tea
Treasure Chest	Oversized: Holds 1,000 Coins
Book (by Topic)	+1 rolls related to topic
Cloak	Stay warm and dry in rain/snow
Manacles	Hard to lockpick
Map (location or region)	+2 rolls to navigate depicted area
Crown	+2 Charisma
Mandolin	Make Music
Flute	Make Music
Harp	Make Music
Trumpet	Announce Yourself

LIVESTOCK
Dog
Cat
Ferret
Falcon

HIRELING	GOLD PER MONTH
Squire	2
Steward	5
Blacksmith	5
Guard	1
Archer	3
Hunter	3
Soldier	2
Jester	1
Servant	1
Chambermaid	2
Nanny	2
Translator	5
Cook	3
Fortune Teller	10
Healer	25
Scholar	2
Architect	10
Illuminator	2
Chaplain	5
Handmaiden	2
Tutor	3
Governess	5
Nurse	2
Wizard	50
Spy	10

Hirelings and Servants may be selected in place of an Item, but they will have a monthly upkeep cost in Gold. Hireling NPCs will have 7 points in their appropriate Primary skills, and 3 points in their Occupation Skill. They will have 2 points to add to their Attribute Scores, appropriate work clothes, and their Occupation Item. Only half of the upkeep cost will be paid out as wages, the rest is for accommodations.

NOBILITY

Name: Level:
Role: Primary Skills:
Title: XP:
Archetype: Gold:

ATTRIBUTES/STATUS

BODY　　　　　　HEALTH

MIND　　　　　　SANITY

SPIRIT　　　　　MORALE

SKILLS

BODY　　**MIND**　　**SPIRIT**
Agility　　Knowledge　　Charisma
Beauty　　Perception　　Empathy
Strength　Technology　　Focus

COMBAT　**STRANGE**　**MARTIAL**
Boxing　　Art　　　　　Dodge
Melee　　Languages　　Parry
Ranged　　Science　　　Strike

PSIONICS　**DIVINE**　**OCCULT**
Clairvoyance　Blessing　　Demonology
Psychokinesis　Exorcism　　Metamorphosis
Telepathy　　Healing　　　Necromancy

LIMITS

ENCUMBRANCE:　　　　DAILY PRAYERS:
MOVE/COMBAT:　　　　SPELL MEMORY:
MOVE/TRAVEL:

ITEMS

Armor:　　　　　Weapon:
Other:
Spells:

31

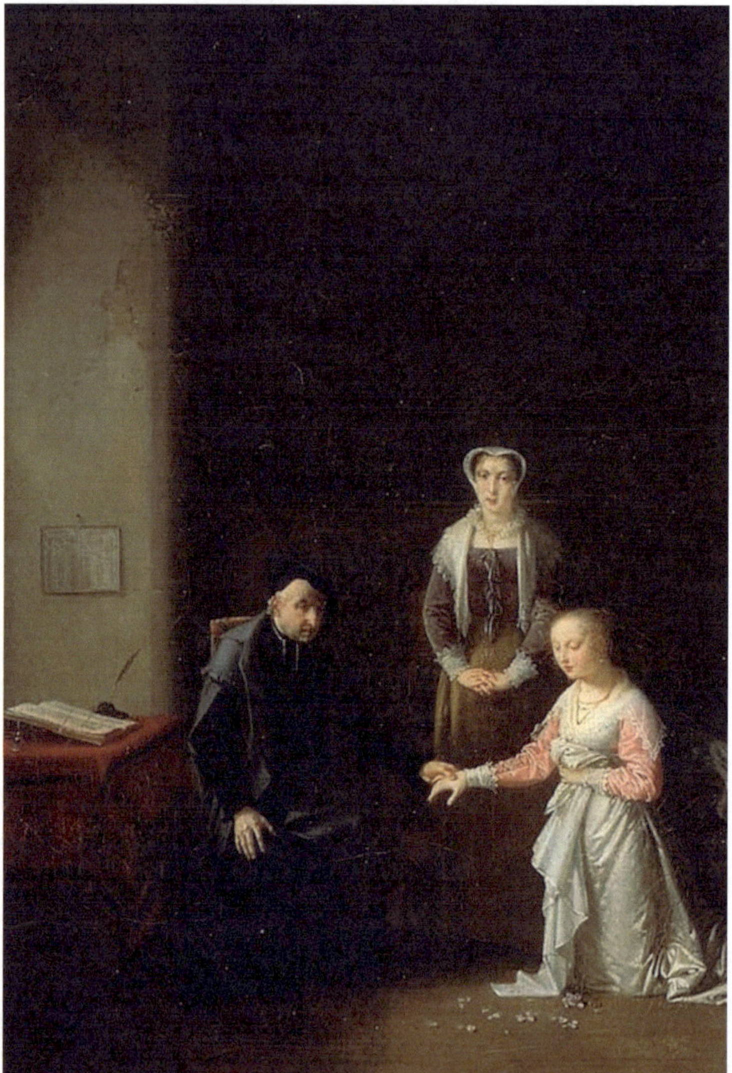

Clergy & Maidens

Clergy and Maidens represent the Church, the dominant institution of the Religious Class. Even though the majority of official ranks within the Church are filled by clergymen, the Maidens in good-standing with Church Doctrine are important pillars of their communities and households. Both will answer the call to public service in times of peril and need.

Characters who begin as Commoners, Nobles, or Outlaws are able to join the Church and enter the Religious Class, either by great deeds of charity, dedication to theological study, or by donating a large tithe to the Church to join a Monastic Order, or to attend a Seminary University. Wizards and Witches are never allowed to join the Church. Starting level Clergy and Maiden Player Characters are assumed to have dedicated themselves to the service of the Church at a young age and have completed their studies, or have otherwise proven themselves to their community.

Where the Nobility is charged with the physical protection of their lands and the people within, to the Church falls the duty to protect humanity from spiritual harm and crisis. Commoners and Outlaws will typically treat Religious characters respectfully, while Nobles view the Church as a rival for power, making public showings of supporting the Church while behind closed doors ever searching for ways to limit the Church's influence on the politics of their Kingdom.

The Church controls vast amounts of wealth, but most of its members are poor. Their needs are cared for in exchange for a lifetime of service and dedication, which can lead outsiders and critics to believe them to be personally profiting from the generosity of their congregations. Certainly this is true in some cases, but in Medieval times, the degree to which people were concerned about the condition of their souls, and the promise of Heaven, is hard for modern people to truly understand. Satan's corrupting influence was as unquestionable and real as the pull of gravity.

Despite the vast treasuries they control, most transactions conducted by the Church Class are made in Silver Coins, or by Loans and promissory notes with flat repayment fees.

Clergy and Maiden Characters receive 5 points to add to skills in their Primary School. These skills cannot be raised higher than +4 with points during Character Creation.

The Player will then select an Occupation the Character holds within the Church. This Occupation will list a skill that the Character receives a +1 bonus to, even if it takes that skill as high as +5, if it is one of their Primary skills.

After the Occupational bonus has been applied, the Character then receives 9 additional points that they may add to skills in their Primary Category, their Occupational skill, or to any skill in the Categories of Body, Mind, Spirit, Combat, and Strange. Skills from outside of their Primary school may not be raised higher than +3 during Character Creation.

CLERGY

Dedicated to lifelong service to the Church, their Flock, and the Salvation of Mankind.

CLASS: Church
PRIMARY SKILLS: Divine

OCCUPATION	BONUS	ITEM
Priest	Blessing+1	Bible (Book)
Exorcist	Exorcism+1	Holy Symbol
Healer	Healing+1	Incense
Acolyte	Beauty+1	Ceremonial Kit
Scholar	Knowledge+1	History Book
Architect	Technology+1	Tool Kit
Orator	Charisma+1	Hat
Confessor	Empathy+1	Lash
Monk	Focus+1	Kit of Choice
Choir	Art+1	Book of Songs
Illuminator	Languages+1	Writing Kit
Friar	Science+1	Gardening Kit
Chaplain	Dodge+1	Medicine Kit
Witchfinder	Telepathy+1	Holy Symbol

STARTING COINS: Spirit+Empathy (Silver)

*Characters that begin as Clergy at starting level of experience are literate, whether or not they have placed points in the Languages Skill.

MAIDEN

Dedicated to lifelong support of the Church, their community, and to the saving of souls.

CLASS: Church
PRIMARY SKILLS: Spirit

OCCUPATION	BONUS	ITEM
Virgin	Blessing+1	Holy Symbol
Exorcist	Exorcism+1	Ceremonial Kit
Healer	Healing+1	Incense
Handmaiden	Beauty+1	Work Outfit
Midwife	Knowledge+1	Medicine Kit
Tutor	Perception+1	History Book
Governess	Technology+1	Lash
Almoner	Charisma+1	Donation Box
Confessor	Empathy+1	
Nun	Focus+1	Medicine Kit
Choir	Art+1	Book of Songs
Nurse	Science+1	Medicine Kit
Oracle	Clairvoyance+1	Bible (Book)
Witchfinder	Telepathy+1	Holy Symbol

STARTING COINS: Spirit x10 (Silver)

*Characters that begin as Church Maidens at starting level of experience are literate, whether or not they have placed points in the Languages Skill.

37

Clergy and Maiden Characters have full access to the abilities they gain if they have points placed in Divine skills, as described in the Rules Handbook.

Clergy Characters begin their adventures with a Church Outfit appropriate to their rank. Only Nuns, Exorcists, Healers, Tutors, Almoners, Confessors, Nurses, and Witchfinders will have a Church outfit from the Maiden Occupations. The remaining Maiden Occupations will start off with a Nice Dress and shoes. They will have the Item listed with their Occupation, and 2 additional selections from Commoner or Church Equipment.

WEAPON	DAMAGE	RANGE
Lash	1 Morale	close/self

EQUIPMENT	DETAILS
Holy Symbol/Jewelry	+1 Exorcism +1 Beauty
Holy Symbol/Cross	+2 Exorcism (Hand Sized)
Ceremonial Kit	+1 Religious Ceremony actions
Writing Kit	+1 Languages for writing actions
Gardening Kit	+2 Garden-related rolls
Medicine Kit	+1 recovery assistance
Incense	+1 Focus while praying
Donation Box	Holds 100 Coins

LIVESTOCK
Cat
Donkey

CHURCH

Name: Level:
Role: Primary Skills:
Occupation: XP:

ATTRIBUTES/STATUS

BODY   HEALTH
MIND   SANITY
SPIRIT   MORALE

SKILLS

BODY   **MIND**   **SPIRIT**
Agility   Knowledge   Charisma
Beauty   Perception   Empathy
Strength   Technology   Focus

COMBAT   **STRANGE**   **MARTIAL**
Boxing   Art   Dodge
Melee   Languages   Parry
Ranged   Science   Strike

PSIONICS   **DIVINE**
Clairvoyance   Blessing
Psychokinesis   Exorcism
Telepathy   Healing

LIMITS

ENCUMBRANCE: DAILY PRAYERS:
MOVE/COMBAT:
MOVE/TRAVEL:

ITEMS

Armor: Weapon:
Other:

39

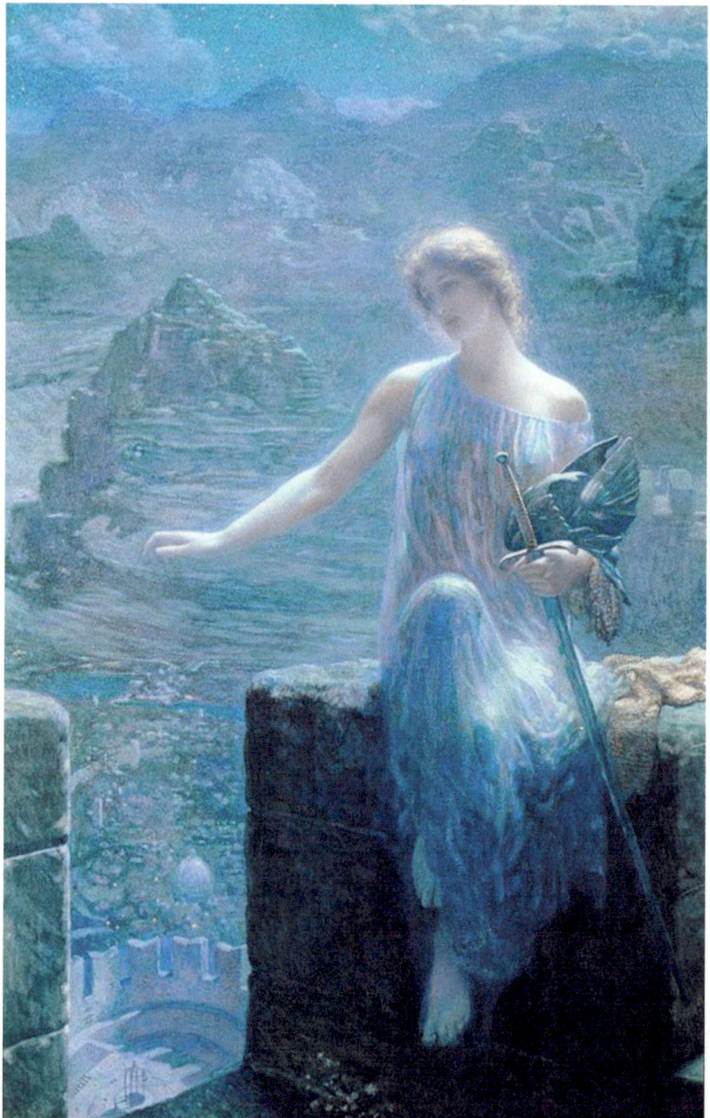

Wizards & Witches

Both feared and admired, respected and reviled, Wizards and Witches exist outside of the Medieval system of Social Class, neither fully Noble nor Outcast, yet with elements of all Classes. Wizards bend reality to their will by the use of Psionics, and future knowledge. They are frequently employed by the Nobility, and the most powerful among them have been able to seize a Noble Title for themselves.

Witches, on the other hand, traffic in the Occult, keeping the company of demons and ghosts, and creating spells of transformation. They are branded as Outlaws by the Church, but to those among the Commoners and Nobility who still respect the Old Ways and have secret pagan beliefs, Witches are every bit respected as the original Religious Class had been before the arrival of the Church. Among the Fairy Folk, Witches are treated as Priestesses, and the Church's clergymen are despised and outlawed in their territories.

Wizard and Witch Characters receive 5 points to add to skills in their Primary school. No Primary Skill may be raised higher than +4 with points during Character Creation.

Once these points have been added, the Player will then select an Occupation for their Character, which applies a +1 Bonus to a specific skill. This bonus can potentially raise a Primary skill as high as +5, if the bonus goes to a skill in that school with enough points placed in it.

Once the Occupational Bonus is applied, Wizard and Witch Characters receive an additional 9 points to add to skills in their Primary Category, their Occupational Skill, or to any skill in the schools of Body, Mind, Spirit, Combat, or Strange. No skill outside of their Primary school may be raised higher than +3 during Character Creation.

Wizards and Witches are paid and conduct transactions with Gold Coins or Favors. Both are literate whether or not they have placed points in the Languages skill.

WIZARD

Half-Huckster, Half-God-Complex, Wizards seek to change the Future they can see coming by imposing their own Vision.

CLASS: Nobility
PRIMARY SKILLS: Psionics

OCCUPATION	BONUS
Astrologer	Clairvoyance+1
Conjurer	Psychokinesis+1
Psychic	Telepathy+1
Diabolist	Demonology+1
Alchemist	Metamorphosis+1
Necromancer	Necromancy+1
Doctor	Healing+1
Sage	Knowledge+1
Engineer	Technology+1
Bard	Art+1
Scribe	Language+1
Inventor	Science+1

STARTING COINS: 10 + Mind + Charisma

WITCH

Pagan blasphemers who keep the traditions of the Old Ways alive, and protect their people in Secret from Fairies and Spirits.

CLASS: Outlaw
PRIMARY SKILLS: Occult

OCCUPATION	BONUS
Seer	Clairvoyance+1
Sorceress	Psychokinesis+1
Psychic	Telepathy+1
Summoner	Demonology+1
Enchantress	Metamorphosis+1
Hag	Necromancy+1
Druidess	Blessing+1
Teacher	Knowledge+1
Ritualist	Art+1
Poet	Languages+1
Naturalist	Science+1
Assassin	Strike+1

STARTING COINS: 10 + Mind + Perception

Wizards and Witches begin the game already knowing a number of spells equal to their Mind Score, which can be chosen from those below, if they have the appropriate skills. These starting spells are Hard to Cast until they can be re-trained. An Occultist can memorize a number of spells equal to their Mind + Knowledge. They can choose to forget their oldest-known spell to learn a new spell when they have reached their Limit.

Wizards and Witches with points in Divine skills will have access to all of the abilities of those skills. They can only Pray (a 2 turn action) for Blessings or Healing a number of times per day equal to their Spirit + Empathy. Once these have been expended, the Character will have to wait 24 hours, or get a full night's rest, before they can use their Divine skills again.

SPELL MEMORY: Mind + Knowledge
DAILY PRAYERS: Spirit + Empathy

DEMONOLOGY SPELLS
Spirit Calling (by Type*)
Spirit Binding (by Type*)
Ward Against Spirits (by Type*)
Astral Travel (Self)
Simple Apparition
False Appearance
Fearful Hysteria

* In Fairy Tale Settings, the Types of Spirits influenced by Demonology include all races of Fairy Folk, plus Cherubs and Nymphs. Demonic Spirits can be easily adapted from other Total Party System game settings. Fairy Folk, Cherubs, and Nymphs will be teleported to the caster's location if the spell is successful, and will be sent back to where they were located prior to the spell's effects if sent back to their point of origin with further spell use.

METAMORPHOSIS SPELLS
Atavistic Traits (Self)
Disguise (Self)
Regeneration (Self)
Wounding (Target or Object)
Change Species (Self, by Type)
Reshaping
Reset Form (Self)

NECROMANCY SPELLS
Shadow Vision
Summon Wisps and Phantoms
Summon Ghost
Ghost Binding
Shadow Sense
Life Drain

Both Wizards and Witches will keep a Grimoire, a special book with enough pages to contain the research notes required to Craft a spell. A Grimoire can hold up to 3 spells worth of research, and can be used by other Wizards and Witches to cut their own crafting time in half to learn one of the spells contained within. Some Witches will refer to their's as a Recipe Book if they favor Metamorphosis over other Occult skills.

Wizards will start with a set of Traveler's Clothes, a Wizard's Costume (Robes), a Grimoire with blank pages, and a Backpack. They may select 1 additional item from Commoner, Nobility, Church, or Magician equipment options.

Witches begin the game with a Peasant Dress with shoes, and a set of Priestess' Robes. They will also have a Grimoire or Recipe Book with blank pages, a Medicine Kit, and 1 item of choice from the Commoner, Church, or Magician equipment options.

WEAPON	DAMAGE	RANGE
Flintlock Pistol	2	4
Flintlock Musket	3	6

ARMOR	DEFENSE	DETAILS
Wizard's Hat	Padded	+1 Charisma
Witch's Hat	Padded	+1 Charisma

EQUIPMENT	DETAILS
Grimoire	holds up to 3 spells
Recipe Book	holds up to 3 spells
Magician's Kit	+1 spell actions
Candlemaker Kit	Makes 10 candles
Gunpowder Kit	Reload Flintlock (1 Turn)
Horn of Buckshot	20 shots with Flintlock
Wizard's Costume	+1 Charisma
Priestess' Robe	+1 Beauty

MAGICIAN

Name: Level:
Role: Primary Skills:
Occupation: XP:

ATTRIBUTES/STATUS

BODY HEALTH

MIND SANITY

SPIRIT MORALE

SKILLS

BODY
Agility
Beauty
Strength

MIND
Knowledge
Perception
Technology

SPIRIT
Charisma
Empathy
Focus

COMBAT
Boxing
Melee
Ranged

STRANGE
Art
Languages
Science

MARTIAL
Dodge
Parry
Strike

PSIONICS
Clairvoyance
Psychokinesis
Telepathy

DIVINE
Blessing
Exorcism
Healing

OCCULT
Demonology
Metamorphosis
Necromancy

LIMITS

ENCUMBRANCE: DAILY PRAYERS:
MOVE/COMBAT: SPELL MEMORY:
MOVE/TRAVEL:

ITEMS

Armor: Weapon:
Other:
Spells:

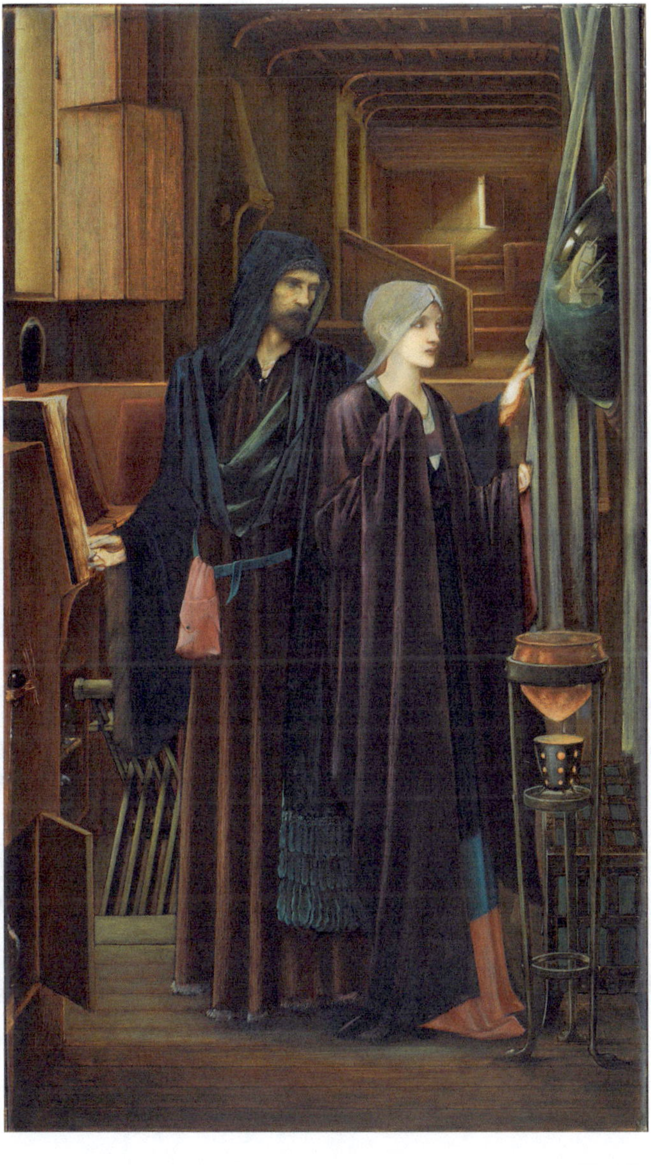

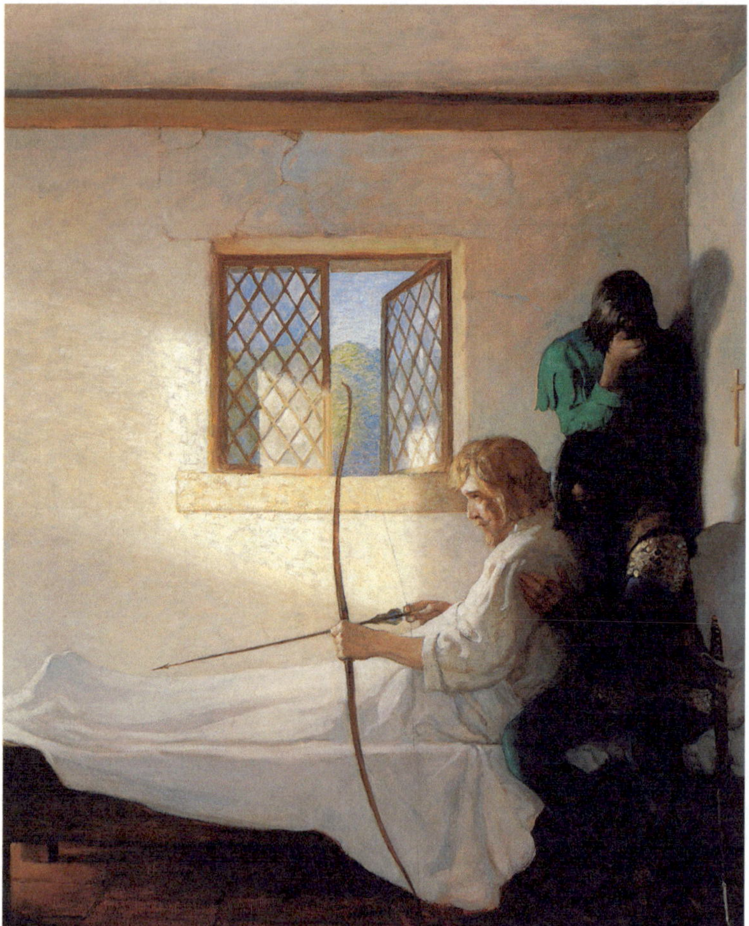

Outlaws

CLASS: Outlaw
PRIMARY SKILLS: Martial

Outlaws, like Wizards and Witches, exist outside of the system of Social Class, living in defiance of the Laws of both Kingdom and Church, whether by circumstance or by choice. Anyone who is expelled from their Social Class by their misdeeds, or has a Bounty placed upon their head by Noble Writ, will become a member of the Outlaw Class: Unable to buy property, unable to do business publicly, unable to seek lawful employment, and constantly on-guard against being spotted by lawmen, bounty hunters, and snitches.

About half of the Commoner Class will see Outlaws as anti-heroes, able to strike back against their oppressors on their behalf. There is an even smaller following of similar-minded people among the Church, who may turn a blind eye and pretend not to notice notorious Outlaws who are known to do good things for their community. But in official capacities, most Commoners and Church members cannot publicly associate with Outlaws, or risk becoming one themselves.

Outlaws come from a variety of Backgrounds, which shapes their Character.

Starting level Outlaws receive 5 points to add to skills in their Primary category of Martial. None of these skills may be raised higher than +4 with points during Character Creation.

Outlaw Characters will have a second category of Primary skills, with the same restrictions, that is determined by their selection of Background. They will have 3 points to add to these skills at this stage of Character Creation.

BACKGROUND	SKILLS	CLOTHES
Criminal	Body	Peasant
Thief	Mind	Dark
Liar	Spirit	Nice
Bandit/Pirate	Combat	Traveler
Spy	Strange	Peasant or Nice
Hypnotist	Psionics	Wizard Costume
Heretic	Divine	Priest Outfit
Warlock	Occult	Dark

Outlaw Characters receive an additional 7 points that they may add to skills in either of their two Primary schools, or to any skills in the schools of Body, Mind, Spirit, Combat, and Strange. Skills outside of their Primary schools cannot be raised higher than +3 during Character Creation.

Outlaws are only automatically literate if they come from the Spy, Heretic, or Warlock background. Otherwise they will have to have at least +1 in the Languages skill to be able to read their native language's written form.

Outlaws trade in all forms of Coin, Barter, and the occasional Favor.

CRIMINAL STARTING COINS: 10 + Mind + Agility (Silver)
THIEF STARTING COINS: Body + Perception (Gold)
LIAR STARTING COINS: 10 + Spirit + Charisma (Gold)
BANDIT STARTING COINS: 10 + Spirit + Strength (Silver)
SPY STARTING COINS: Mind x10 (Gold)
HYPNOTIST STARTING COINS: Spirit x10 (Silver)
HERETIC STARTING COINS: Spirit + Perception (Copper)
WARLOCK STARTING COINS: Mind + Focus (Copper)

Outlaws of the Warlock Background will know spells as per the rules for Wizards and Witches.

Outlaw Characters begin with an outfit of clothing of the style listed with their Background, including shoes or boots as appropriate. They may select 3 items from Commoner or Outlaw equipment.

ARMOR	DEFENSE	DETAILS
Leather Jacket	Plated	+1 Charisma
Chainmail	Plated	Concealable
Dark Clothing	None	+2 Stealth actions

WEAPON	DAMAGE	RANGE
Blowgun	Poison	3
Dart (thrown)	Poison	2
Throwing Knife	1 or Poison	2 or close
Health Poison	5	ingest or weapon
Sanity Poison	3 Sanity	ingest or weapon
Morale Poison	3 Morale	ingest or weapon
Sleep Poison	Sleep 8 hours	ingest or weapon
Sword	2	close
Spear	2	2 or close
Crossbow	2	4
Bomb	4 to range 2	2 (3 Turn Fuse)

EQUIPMENT	DETAILS
Poison Bottle	Holds 5 Doses of same type
Box of Darts	10 Darts
Quiver of Bolts	12 Bolts for Crossbow
Lockpick	+2 Pick Locks
Eye-Mask	+2 Conceal Identity
Treasure Chest	Oversized, Holds 1,000 Coins

LIVESTOCK
Dog
Horse
Donkey

OUTLAW

Name: Level:
Role: Primary Skills:
Background: Primary Skills:

ATTRIBUTES/STATUS

BODY HEALTH

MIND SANITY

SPIRIT MORALE

SKILLS

BODY	MIND	SPIRIT
Agility	Knowledge	Charisma
Beauty	Perception	Empathy
Strength	Technology	Focus

COMBAT	STRANGE	MARTIAL
Boxing	Art	Dodge
Melee	Languages	Parry
Ranged	Science	Strike

PSIONICS	DIVINE	OCCULT
Clairvoyance	Blessing	Demonology
Psychokinesis	Exorcism	Metamorphosis
Telepathy	Healing	Necromancy

LIMITS

ENCUMBRANCE: DAILY PRAYERS:
MOVE/COMBAT: SPELL MEMORY:
MOVE/TRAVEL:

ITEMS

Armor: Weapon:
Other:
Spells:
XP:

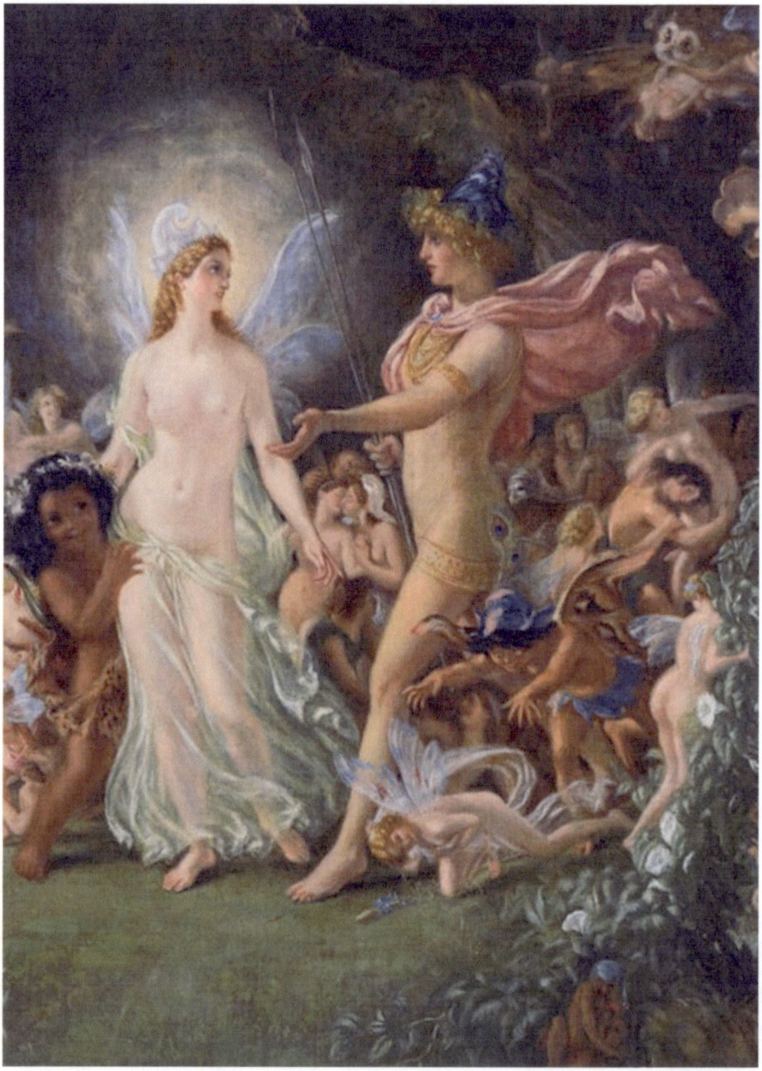

Fairy Folk

In game terms, beings such as Ghosts and Inhuman Spirits can be described as beings of pure psychic energy. The Fairy Folk are another form of Inhuman Spirits. In their case, made from pure psychic matter. They are not flesh and bone, as you and I, and neither are they made of wood or stone or smoke or water, or any other material substance that makes up our world. And yet they are every bit as physically real as any mortal man.

There are five races of Fairy. They have been known by different names in different lands to different people, but there always are five different kinds of them that fit into these five Roles. They are each different from the other, and though they never war among one another, they all seem to dislike each other. Yet they are all Fairy, and have more in common than they do not.

Fairies are all immortal beings. They can be damaged by attacks that damage their Status, but do not recover until that Status becomes Incapacitated, at which point the fairy will vanish as they reflexively teleport back to their home dimension to heal. 28 days later they will appear in the middle of whichever Fairy Circle happens to be closest to where they became Incapacitated. They cannot be healed with Divine, Occult, or Psionic means. Though they do not bleed, their wounds will remain with them, including any debilitating effects, until they become Incapacitated. When they reappear in the Fairy Circle after 28 days, they will have recovered all lost Status levels, of all types. They will have any clothes or items they were carrying at the time that they vanished to recover.

Fairy Folk do not need to breathe, except to draw breath for speaking, and they do not need to eat, though they seem to enjoy doing so, and can eat anything that is vaguely edible, even if it may be toxic to Humans. All that is required is that it be some form of plant, animal, or fungus, in order for a Fairy to digest it. Some can be surprisingly good cooks, but non-Fairies should be careful when eating their food that it is not accidentally poisonous. They do not need to sleep either, but can make themselves do so with a Hard Spirit+Focus action if they want to dream. They seldom sleep longer than 4 hours at a time.

Fairies are also immune to all poisons and disease, and take half damage from cold and fire. Metamorphosis spells cast upon them, if successful, will work as intended, but they will still be made out of the same psychic material that forms their original bodies, and will automatically revert to their original form at the next sunset.

Fairies can be unexpectedly teleported away from where they are, and may be returned on a whim, if they are summoned by someone using Demonology spells to call on fairy spirits, or that Character by their name. They can be effected by Ward spells, and must make a Very difficult Mind+Focus action to force themselves to enter Holy Ground.

Fairies do need to drink fresh water, but only half as much as a human requires.

When Fairies from all five races gather in a Fairy Circle they can open a portal of light that leads to their home dimension. This requires all Fairies involved (at least 1 from each race) to succeed at a Hard Spirit+Psychokinesis action as they focus their psychic energies together to open a passage between worlds. Fairies call these portals "Trods". They will stay open for 1 minute for each fairy who participated in opening it, but if even one of them failed their Psychokinesis roll, the Trod will not open, and the Fairy Circle will go dormant until the next full moon.

Fairies of all kinds, even if they spend most of their time above ground, keep their dwellings in subterranean caverns and mines, or beneath small constructed hills and mounds called Cairns or Barrows. They will live together in groups ranging in size from the equal of a small Human village, up to a small Human city, depending on both the size of the available space, and the size of the Fairies that inhabit it.

Most Fairy settlements are dominated by a single Fairy Race, with some Fairy Friend races living among them. Only the rare Fairy City will have a diverse mix of Fairy Folk and Friends. These often serve as capitals of the great Fairy Kingdoms.

All Fairy Cairns, Barrows, and the Fairy Castle guarding a Fairy City, will have somewhere within them a small chamber in which an altar is placed for a Human sleeping in stasis to be placed upon. The Human is always taken from the Commoner Class, and must consent to be put into an ageless sleep of up to 100 years before they Fairies will awaken them and replace them with a new Human dreamer. Somehow the dreams of the sleeping Human allow the Fairies that live near there to be able to sleep and dream. Without a Human dreamer, they will fail any attempt to make themselves go to sleep. They will also fail attempts to sleep and dream if they are more than 100 miles away from the nearest Cairn, Barrow, or Fairy Castle. The Human dreamer will not age while asleep upon the altar, and will not require food or drink to survive. They will experience time pass quickly within the shared dreamscape of the Fairies who depend on them. After awakening, they are often rewarded handsomely.

The Humans used in this manner must be placed upon the altar on one of the Solstice nights, and the next dreamer must be placed on the opposite Solstice as their predecessor, sometimes depriving Fairy communities of the ability to dream for several months between dreamers, depending on the timing of the previous Human's awakening. A Human that has served the Fairies in this manner is considered Fairy Nobility.

Fairy Circles are naturally occurring patterns in foliage and landscape that form mysterious rings found in wilderness settings, away from Human settlements (by at least 12 miles). These tiny clear patches are the opposite of Haunts. These are places where magic has been used often and/or to great effect, leaving behind a thinner barrier between the Earth and the Heavens. Using any Occult Spell, or Divine or Psionic ability, in a Fairy Circle receives a +2 bonus towards its success. Humans and Inhumans alike.

Fairy Kingdoms co-exist alongside Human Kingdoms, occupying different parts of the same physical territories and typically with radically different borders. Most Humans, except Witches and pagans, are totally unaware that the Fairy Kingdoms are there at all, but most Fairies are painfully aware of their neighboring humans.

Human roads will sometimes cut obtrusively across Fairy Lands, but the roads they use are Hard to perceive with mortal eyes, twisting through forests and around and under mountains, linking the Cairns and Fairy Cities together across their domains.

Only Male Pixies, and Goblins of any gender, will try to live in and around human settlements. Male Pixies will build small hidden homes near human villages and homesteads, to secretly lend assistance to any Human Commoners or Church-members in the area whom they deem worthy. Goblins will build elaborate lairs inside the sewers and abandoned cellars and catacombs beneath human towns and cities. Goblins will keep a Human dreamer on an altar of their own within their lair, like with any Cairn or Barrow.

The only functional difference between a Cairn and a Barrow is who is using it. Both are artificial mounds or small hills that sit atop a network of artificial tunnels and chambers where the fairies dwell. Elves and Female Pixies call their's Cairns, while the Gnomes and Ogres call them Barrows.

Fairies of any type may live in a natural Cavern, and Gnomes and Goblins will also live in Mines, both abandoned and active. The size of the community is dependent on the available space. Pixies tend to prefer Caverns close to the surface, with openings large enough for them to fly through.

Fairy Cities are not commonplace, like Human cities, and are located in the deep wilderness, far from any human habitation (by at least 300 miles). The homes of its inhabitants will be underground, but much of the city may be located on the surface, in the depths of an untamed forest, on a tiny island, on a mountain top, or tucked away into a canyon or cliffside. Exceptionally large Caverns and cave networks can also be the site of a Fairy City. Most Fairy Cities will have a Fairy Castle in them or nearby, where the Fairy King and Queen of their realm dwell. Only Fairy Folk, Fairy Friends, former Dreamers, and Shapeshifters in the Fairy Nobility can become a Fairy King or Queen and rule the wilderness.

Cities without Fairy Castles are never capitals of Fairy Kingdoms, and will be ruled by an Archduke or Archduchess under the authority of the Kingdom. Perhaps 1 in 5 Fairy Cities will not have a Castle.

Most Fairy Cities have a cosmopolitan mixture of different Fairy Folk and their allies, each with their own area of the city designed to suit their lifestyle needs. The sole exceptions are Goblin Cities, which can grow out of Goblin Lairs below the largest of Human Metropoli. They do not have their own Fairy Castle, and are generally considered to be anarchist Outlaws outside of the jurisdiction of whichever Fairy Kingdom they are located within. Other Fairy Folk are as welcome here as they are in other Fairy Cities, but the Goblin Cities are designed solely for Goblin comfort and tastes. Other Fairies dwelling here are always a little uncomfortable, making them edgier than they would be under normal circumstances.

Each Fairy Folk Role has its own special abilities and Limits. Every Fairy Role has an associated school of Primary skills, and Characters will also select an Archetype that goes with their Role, as well as a Psionics Skill they have natural talent with, to further define their abilities. Different Fairy Races/Roles belong to different Social Classes within Fairy Society, which other non-Fairy Inhumans, and Human Witches, belong to.

Fairy Folk have the same number of Attribute points as Human Characters at starting level of experience. They determine Status levels in the same manner as Humans as well (Attribute+2).

Their Role will determine their Fairy Social Class, how their Skill points are allocated, and will determine their Limit values, starting item options, and any special abilities their Fairy race possesses.

ROLE	SKILLS	CLASS	PAGE
Elf	Psionics	Nobility	73
Pixie	Divine	Church	78
Gnome	Strange	Commoner	89
Goblin	Occult	Outlaw	98
Ogre	Martial	Commoner	105

Fairy Folk Characters receive 5 points to add to skills in their Primary school of skills as determined by their Role. Skills in this school may not be raised higher than +4 with points during Character Creation.

Fairy Folk Characters will receive a +1 Bonus to one of the Psionics Skills to reflect their Talent, even if it raises that skill as high as +5, if it is in their Primary school.

TALENT	BONUS
Soothsaying	Clairvoyance+1
Trickery	Psychokinesis+1
Mindreading	Telepathy+1

Fairy Folk Characters will also receive a +1 Bonus to a skill determined by their chosen Archetype, even if it raises that skill as high as +5.

The Fairy Character then receives an additional 3 points to add to any skill in their Primary School, their Talent or Archetype Skills, or from the schools of Body, Mind, Spirit, Combat, Strange, or Psionics. No skill from outside of their Primary school may be raised higher than +3.

ELF

Lords and Ladies of the Fairy Kingdoms, obligated to uphold the Old Ways and the Old Laws, and experience life, music, and love.

CLASS: Nobility
PRIMARY SKILLS: Psionics

ARCHETYPE	BONUS
Acrobat	Agility+1
Courtier	Beauty+1
Adventurer	Strength+1
Philosopher	Knowledge+1
Ranger	Perception+1
Troubadour	Charisma+1
Hermit	Focus+1
Fighter	Boxing+1
Swashbuckler	Melee+1
Juggler	Ranged+1
Composer	Art+1
Vagabond	Languages+1
Knight	Strike+1
Messenger	Dodge+1
Angel	Blessing+1
Healer	Healing+1
Illusionist	Demonology+1
Transmuter	Metamorphosis+1
Witchdoctor	Necromancy+1

Elves have a near-human appearance, and with the right clothing and a wide-brimmed hat or hood, they can conceal their Inhuman nature on a casual inspection with an Average Body+Beauty action before entering a location.

They stand between four and a half to six feet tall, and are typically slender in build and features. They have large, pointed, occassionally wolf-like ears, and will have bright eyes, sometimes with exotic colors. Their hair colors trend towards the lighter blondes and reds, and occasional brunette.

Elves have a greater amount of gender parity than Humans of the medieval era. Both males and females will hold positions of authority. All Elves have some type of Noble Title, but how they rank among each other is hard even for they to fathom. Any Elf with family ties to the King or Queen may take the Title of Sidhe, and serve as an emissary for their sovereign until they have a chance to battle it out with the other Sidhe to seize the throne on those rare times when one becomes vacant.

Elves can reproduce periodically, once a century or so, in a fashion not entirely unlike the human process of creating a new human. Elves cannot have offspring with human lovers, they must mate with another Elf to create progeny. Elves remain as children until they reach adulthood after a century or two. They do not have an equivalent of the human teenage adolescence, they go straight from children to adults seemingly overnight, with little to no indication it is about to happen.

Elves have sensitive, wolf-like senses. They receive a bonus 1d6 to their dice pool when making actions to use their Perception where their sense of smell or hearing are involved. They also have excellent nightvision in low-moonlight conditions.

Elves have the following Limits:

ENCUMBRANCE: Body +. Strength + Psychokinesis
MOVE/COMBAT: Body + Agility + Telepathy
MOVE/TRAVEL: Body + Strength + Clairvoyance

Elves conduct trade with shared Oaths, the promise of Favors, Gemstones, and Silver Coins.

STARTING COINS: Mind x50 (Silver)

Elves start the game with 1 set of Elf Clothes of their choice, and 4 items of choice from the Commoner, Noble, Magician, and Elf equipment options.

ELF CLOTHES	DETAILS
Fancy Suit	+1 Charisma
Fancy Gown	+1 Beauty
Fancy Robes	+1 Public Speaking
Fancy Cloak	+1 Agility
Gossamer Dress	+1 Beauty
Work Outfit	+1 Conceal identity
Jewelry Outfit	+2 Beauty
Rogue's Outfit	+1 Charisma
Fancy Hat*	Padded Armor Defense
Ceremonial Armor	Padded Armor Defense
Half-Plate Cuirass	Plated Armor Defense

*A Fancy Hat worn with Padded or Plated armor gives the wearer Full Suit Armor Defense.

PIXIE

The Classic small, winged, and cheerful Fairies, Pixies are a people divided by their devotion to either the Church or the Old Ways.

CLASS: Church/Religious
PRIMARY SKILLS: Divine

Pixies are currently split by a several century old feud between those who have converted to the teachings of the Church, and those who have remained true to the Old Ways of Fairy. Church Pixies are known as Garden Fairies, and the Old Ways Pixies are known as Wild Fairies. Most, but not all, of the Garden Fairies are male Pixies, and most, but not all, of the Wild Fairies are female Pixies, and they have different Archetypes.

GARDEN FAIRIES:

ARCHETYPE	BONUS
Herald	Knowledge+1
Cobbler	Technology+1
Advocate	Empathy+1
Gardener	Focus+1
Wrestler	Boxing+1
Artisan	Art+1
Illuminator	Languages+1
Crusader	Parry+1
Baptist	Blessing+1
Healer	Necromancy+1

WILD FAIRIES:

ARCHETYPE	BONUS
Courier	Agility+1
Maiden	Beauty+1
Shepherd	Perception+1
Envoy	Charisma+1
Explorer	Science+1
Hunter	Strike+1
Daredevil	Dodge+1
Druidess	Healing+1
Priestess	Demonology+1
Enchantress	Metamorphosis+1

Pixies look like small Elves or Humans that stand between one and three feet tall. Their females tend to range more between one and two feet, and their males between two and three feet in height. All Pixies have insect-like wings sprouting from between their shoulder-blades. Garden Pixies swear a Vow to the Church to conceal and never use their wings to fly. Pixie wings are Easy to conceal.

Pixies have traditionally been known for being a cheerful and carefree people, who watch over and protect Fairy Rings and Cairns from unwanted intrusion. They are often attractive by human standards, though they are not "romantically compatible" with humans unless they have been transformed in size with the use of Metamorphosis spells. Wild Pixies wear tiny, colorful outfits, or more often than not, they wear next to nothing at all. They prefer outfits that leave their wings unobstructed, and will remain airborne most of the day, fluttering around a few feet above the ground.

Church Pixies have rejected their traditional ways, to embrace the stoicism and self-discipline of a life lived in service to God. These Pixies not only refuse to use their wings, keeping them folded down and hidden beneath their clothes, they have also adopted the styles of dress preferred by Human members of the Church, sewing tiny priests uniforms and the darkly colored, skin covering dresses worn by Human Maidens. Church Pixies take their vows and their duties extremely seriously, and can become annoyed or angry when in the presence of someone who is behaving in a frivolous or blasphemous manner. Church Pixies try to stay out of sight during the daylight hours, and will emerge to do their good deeds after sunset.

Pixies cannot wear functional Armors of the kinds employed by larger races, as the materials would have to be so lightweight they would not offer any significant protection to their wearer. The small size of the Pixies, however, gives them far more options to find effective Cover, and their size and reflexes make them hard to hit, giving them an equivalent to a defense of "Magical Armor", (Very Difficult).

Pixie weapons are similarly too flimsy to be used under normal combat circumstances. Pixie Weapons will only do damage to Humans and larger Fairies and supernatural creatures if they have been coated with poison. They will also set up elaborate traps or contraptions that make use of normal sized weapons, to discourage and repel unwanted visitors in their territory.

Pixies' small size gives them a bonus of 1D6 to their dice pool when making rolls to determine if they can successfully hide and conceal themselves from a casual inspection.

The Pixies' greatest ability, in the eyes of those who admire them, are their wings. They will have an insect-like appearance, resembling the wings of dragonflies, butterflies, moths, wasps, and other flying insectoids. These wings are delicate, have a wingspan twice as wide as the Pixie is tall, and can be easily and comfortably folded up against their back, able to be concealed under their clothing at Easy difficulty.

These wings allow the Pixie to fly, up to an altitude equal to their Body Score x100 feet. They can hover in place, take off and land with no need for a runway or great height to launch from, and can accelerate up to a number of miles per hour equal to their Body Score x10.

Pixies reproduce in the Spring. After mating, the female will lay a single Pixie egg within the cup of a flower's bulb, from which a fully formed miniature Pixie will emerge a few weeks later. They will only stand about 6 to 7 inches tall after hatching, but within three days they will grow to their full adult height. The Garden Fairies and the Wild Fairies will gather together in the fields between their territories around Easter, to mate and ensure a new harvest of Pixies will be born.

Pixies use the following Limit values:

*ENCUMBRANCE: 1+ Psychokinesis
MOVE/COMBAT: Body + Agility + Psychokinesis
MOVE/TRAVEL: Body + Strength + Psychokinesis
MOVE/FLIGHT: Body + Agility + Psychokinesis

*Most regular-sized items are Oversized for Pixies to carry

Wild Fairies do not use coins or money, they conduct all transactions with shared Oaths and promise of Favors. Garden Fairies will honor the same kind of agreements, but their proximity to Humans has forced them to adopt the use of Copper Coins for payments and purchase of goods.

CHURCH PIXIE
STARTING COINS: 10 + Spirit + Technology (Copper)

A Pixie's strength is relative to their size, and they are extremely limited in what forms of items they may wear or carry with them. The majority of objects designed for humans to pick up casually will almost always be considered Oversized for Pixies to handle. Even some lightweight pocket-sized items humans carry casually will be too large and cumbersome for the smaller Wild Fairies. A Pixie's Encumbrance is strictly for items that are sized appropriately for their use. Many normal types of equipment options can have a Tiny variant, built for Pixies, but some types of gear, like weapons, will not retain their full-sized capabilities. Pixies have no equivalent to pocket-sized items. Worn items count as 0 Encumbrance.

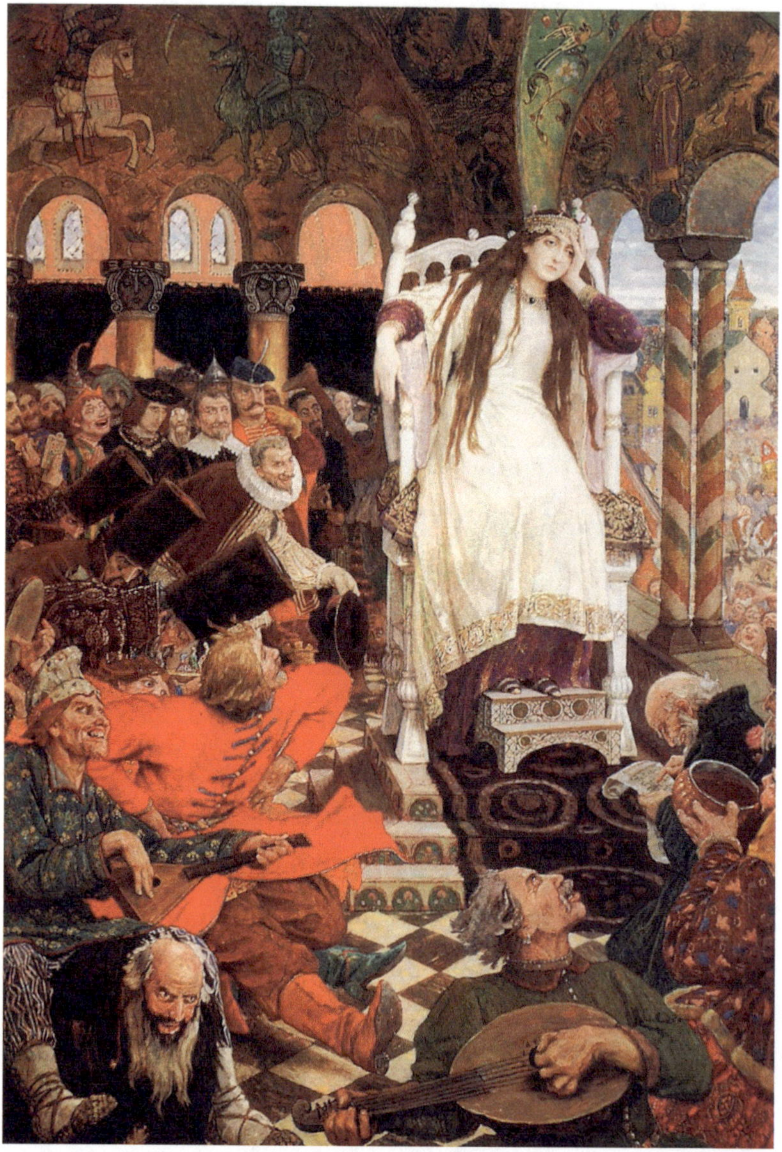

Tiny Items

Wild Fairies start off with 1 item of choice from the Tiny options.

Garden Fairies begin the game with a set of Tiny Clothes of their choice, and 1 additional Tiny item.

TINY CLOTHES	DETAILS
Tiny Gossamer Dress	+1 Beauty
Tiny Woodland Outfit	+1 stealth in foliage
Tiny Nice Gown	+1 Beauty
Tiny Jester Costume	+1 Charisma
Tiny Work Uniform	+1 Focus
Tiny Priest Outfit	+1 Charisma
Tiny Nun Robe	+1 Empathy
Tiny Hat	+1 Charisma
Tiny Cloak	+1 Parry

TINY WEAPONS	DAMAGE	RANGE
Tiny Spear	by Poison	1
Tiny Sword	by Poison	close
Tiny Bow	by Poison	2
Hatchet (2+ ft. tall only)	1	close
Health Poison	5	
Sanity Poison	3 Sanity	
Morale Poison	3 Morale	
Sleep Poison	sleep 8 hours	
Vision Poison	+1 Clairvoyance	

TINY ACCESSORIES*	DETAILS
Tiny Shield	+1 Dodge, +1 Parry
Tiny Quiver of Arrows	6 Tiny Arrows
Vial of Poison	1 Dose
Tiny Torch	half hour of light
Tiny Tool Kit	+2 repairs
Tiny Fire Kit	start a fire
Tiny Makeup Kit	+1 Beauty
Tiny Jewelry	+ Beauty
Tiny Book (by topic)	+1 actions involving topic

TINY LIVESTOCK
Squirrel
Rabbit
Fox
Toad
Bat

*Other human sized items may have a Tiny-sized variant with the approval of the Game Master.

GNOME

Short in stature but great in intellect, Gnomes are students of nature, and the builders of the future.

CLASS: Commoner
PRIMARY SKILLS: Strange

ARCHETYPE	BONUS
Jeweler	Agility+1
Miner	Strength+1
Expert	Knowledge+1
Surveyor	Perception+1
Machinist	Technology+1
Toymaker	Charisma+1
Custodian	Empathy+1
Sentinel	Focus+1
Pugilist	Boxing+1
Burglar	Melee+1
Musketeer	Ranged+1
Sculptor	Art+1
Archivist	Languages+1
Professor	Science+1
Mercenary	Parry+1
Bombmaker	Dodge+1
Physician	Healing+1
Alchemist	Metamorphosis+1
Mortician	Necromancy+1

Gnomes resemble humans closely, but stand between three and a half to four and a half feet tall. They are sturdy, robust Fairy Folk with what can be described as a "peasant look" to their features, and style of dress. Gnomes practice even more gender equality than Elves, and communities of Gnomes will be clannish in their attitudes towards rival Barrows and other Gnome settlements. Each community will have a particular style of fashion and hairdressing that all members of the community will conform to. All the make Gnomes will wear the same outfit, and all the females the same type of dress, the only difference will be color variations of the specific garments and how those colors may be matched. If the males in a community grow out their beards, then they all grow out their beards. If they shave their faces, they all shave their faces. Do the Gnome women wear their hair short, or up in an elaborate twist of hair, or do they grow it long and let it hang loose? Do the Gnome women wear hats? What style of hat do the men wear? On and on go the ways that Gnomes will overthink and conform to community standards.

Gnomes are more sophisticated even than Wizards, with machinery and manufacturing processes centuries ahead of anything found elsewhere in the world, hidden within their Barrows and Caverns. They understand metallurgy and hydraulics, coal-fired steam-engines and gear timing mechanisms. They build the best clocks and toys to be found, and they are beginning to experiment with the concept of assembly lines. Their technologies are not as reliable and effective as those that humans will one day build using the principles the Gnomes are developing today, but they enjoy a lifestyle that is far closer to the Modern than to the Medieval.

Gnome parents will put a great deal of planning and preparation into the decision for a Gnome couple to have a child. They will spend months, if not years, haggling in meetings over what they want the child to be like, when to have them, where to place the nursery, what colors to paint the room, what sort of schooling shall it receive when it's old enough, and on and on, until one night, while both of them are asleep at the same time, an infant Gnome will appear in their crib and start crying. Gnome children reach adulthood at the same rate of development as human children.

Gnomes will receive a thorough education during their childhood. All Gnomes are literate regardless of if they have points in the Languages skill or not. They will have a better grasp of Human history than other Fairies as well.

While sinister Gnomes certainly exist, the average Gnome is altruistic in nature, they simply have little time in their lives for the shenanigans of other Fairy Folk, or the backwardness of Humankind. This gives them a tendency to be short-tempered, dismissive, and rude towards anyone who isn't a Gnome of their specific community, with the sole exception of Wizards, whom they share a common vision for the future with.

While the Gnomes share some surface-level similarities with Church Pixies, Gnomes find them intolerable wannabes, and remain faithful to the Old Ways. They are focused on uncovering new knowledge, new discoveries, and new inventions to make life better for future generations of Fairy.

Despite being so much shorter on average than humans, their sturdy body structure makes them capable of handling and carrying most normal-sized items. They cannot handle two-handed melee weapons built for humans, and all their clothing and armor must be tailor-made to fit them in order to gain any benefits from wearing it.

Gnomes will spend about half of their lifetime underground, on average. They're not particularly in love with the sky, but they aren't afraid of it either. They are, however, quite prodigious as diggers, excavators, and miners. If they have the proper tools, they will have a per turn MOVE/DIGGING Limit that measures the number of ten-foot spaces a Gnome can dig a tunnel through soft materials such as soil and clay, as well as sand and gravel, though these substances will shift to fill in empty spaces below them and collapse the tunnel behind the Gnome as they Move. Digging through softer rocks like chalk or limestone will reduce their Digging Move by half (rounded down, minimum of 1). Digging through hard rock and cement blocks drops their Move/Digging to 1.

Gnomes have a sensitivity to vibrations. They can detect movement with no penalty to Perception in complete darkness, with a range in 10 foot spaces equal to their Mind + Perception + Clairvoyance.

Gnomes use the following Limit values:

ENCUMBRANCE: Body + Strength + Psychokinesis
MOVE/COMBAT: Body + Agility
MOVE/TRAVEL: Body + Strength
MOVE/DIGGING: Strength + Clairvoyance

Gnomes conduct business in all manner of Coins, but favor Gold above all others, as well as gemstones, the use of contracts, and usury.

STARTING COINS: Mind x10 (Gold) + Spirit x3 (Silver)

Gnomes will begin the game with a set of clothes of a peasant style agreed upon by their Fairy community, either a Work Outfit or a Dress. They will also have a pair of boots (all genders), and males will have a Fancy Hat (see Elf items).

They will also select 4 items from either the human Commoner, Magician, or Gnome equipment options. Female Gnomes may select a Fancy Hat as one of their selections if their community agrees.

WEAPONS	DAMAGE	RANGE
Pickaxe (digging tool)	2	close
Power-Claw	3	close
Flamethrower	2 per Turn	2
Flintlock Pistol	2	4
Flintlock Musket	3	6
Cannon (Oversized)	5	10
Bomb	4 to range 2	2 (3 Turn Fuse)

EQUIPMENT	DETAILS
Flamethrower Bottle	Oil for 10 Turns of use
Gunpowder Kit	Reload Flintlock (1 Turn)
Horn of Buckshot	20 shots with Flintlock
Cannon Ball + Powder	2 Turns to reload. Oversized
Headlantern (Hat)	beam of light range 2
Wristwatch	accurate time-keeping
Clockwork Toy	operates for 5 minutes
Clockwork Key	resets a Clockwork's power
IndustrialTool Kit	+3 Repair actions
Miner's Tool Kit	digging tools for soil and rock

LIVESTOCK
Ferret
Badger
Goat
Donkey

GOBLIN

Outlaws of the Fairy Folk, Goblins dwell in dark corners and deep dungeons, ready to overwhelm any who dare intrude on them.

CLASS: Outlaw
PRIMARY SKILLS: Occult

ARCHETYPE	BONUS
Creeper	Agility+1
Hobgoblin	Beauty+1
Appraiser	Knowledge+1
Lookout	Perception+1
Fence	Technology+1
Robber	Melee+1
Sniper	Ranged+1
Vandal	Art+1
Researcher	Languages+1
Looter	Dodge+1
Assassin	Strike+1
Shaman	Demonology+1
Surgeon	Metamorphosis+1
Witchdoctor	Necromancy+1

Goblins have the most diverse range of sizes and appearances of any of the Fairy Folk, standing between two and a half to five feet tall, with both slender and robust builds, and some facial feature or another that is distinctly rodent-like. They will also possess pointed ears like an Elf's, and their skin colors are alway sickly shades of green, gray, or blue. Of all the Fairy Folk, they spend the largest amount of time underground, preferring to only come to the surface at night, if they must. Most Goblins have some degree of agoraphobia, in regards to being under an open sky.

Due to an insult levied many thousands of years ago, Goblins have been declared as Outlaws in both Fairy and Human Kingdoms. Goblins raise neither Cairn nor Barrow, the few who still live away from the human cities are found in the deepest of Caverns and Mines, where even other Fairy will not go. The bulk of their race have long since migrated to live in the subsurface levels, tunnels, and sewers found beneath major human settlements, such as towns and cities.

Goblins must survive by conducting raids on surface dwelling Humans, and other Inhuman peoples, and by conducting trade amongst themselves, often involving the black market or thieves guild of whichever town or city they dwell beneath, if the humans have enough love of vice.

Goblins have excellent vision in darkness, needing only the faintest amount of light to see without penalty. They do not like bright indoor lights, or sunshine, receiving a +2 to the difficulty of Perception actions that rely on sight while in a well-lit space, or in daylight.

Goblins have few other abilities outside of those possessed by all Fairy Folk. Their affinity for Occult skills, however, gives them access to a broad range of potential powers, especially through the use of Metamorphosis. The powers of Illusion provided by Demonology are of great use to Goblins skilled in it, and many a Goblin lair or dungeon is guarded by zombies raised with the art of Necromancy. On top of these talents, many Goblins will be accomplished thieves, bandits, and smugglers, contributing greatly to the crime rates of any settlement that they live under.

Goblins have the following Limits:

ENCUMBRANCE: Body + Strength + Psychokinesis
MOVE/COMBAT: Body + Agility + Strike
MOVE/TRAVEL: Body + Strength

Goblins will reproduce in a fashion similar to humans, but only the tallest among the Goblin women (four and a half feet or taller) are capable of giving birth to a full litter of Goblin pups. Goblins are born in litters of between 4 and 8, with the record holder being a complete dozen. They will grow up over the course of just a handful of years to join Goblin society.

Goblin females who become pregnant and are not large enough to handle the litter, will give birth to a single offspring who murdered and ate their littermates in the womb, and are born at such a size that their mother will become Incapacitated and teleport away. These children look like oversized Goblin pups at first, but they will reach adulthood in half the time, and will be of monstrous size and disposition. These offspring are known as Trolls, and are detailed in the chapter on Magical Creatures in this Handbook.

Goblins can use human sized objects, but not two-handed weapons, or carry oversized items.

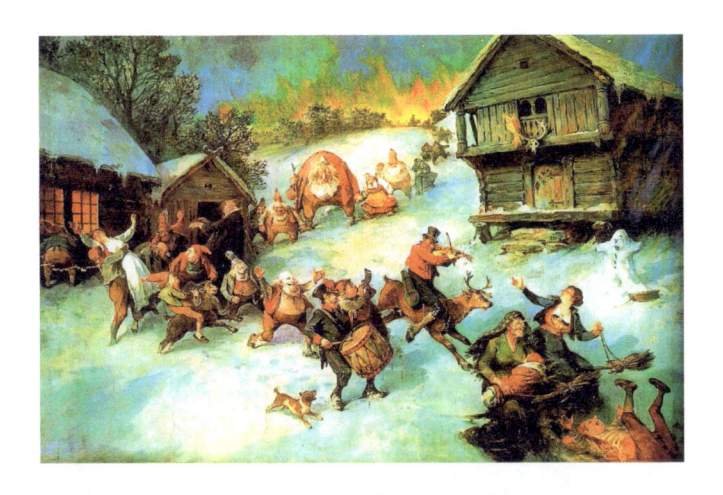

Goblins who have points in the Beauty skill are known as Hobgoblins. They tend to be taller, between five to five and a half feet tall, and will look like Elves, but with darker hair and the same sickly skin coloration of other Goblins.

Goblins begin the game with a set of clothes cobbled together from bits and pieces of different garments of different styles and coloring, favoring darker colors and eye-catching patterns. They will also select 3 items of choice from the human Commoner, Magician, and Outlaw equipment options. Goblins may not take Livestock. They have a +2 to the difficulty of any Animal Handling actions they may attempt.

Goblins trade in Silver Coins, precious Gemstones, and with promise of Favors.

STARTING COINS: Mind + Melee (Silver)

OGRE

Misunderstood by Human and Fairy alike, Ogres have gained an unfair reputation.

CLASS: Commoner
PRIMARY SKILLS: Martial

ARCHETYPE	BONUS
Brute	Strength+1
Tactician	Knowledge+1
Ranger	Perception+1
Mason	Technology+1
Executioner	Empathy+1
Officer	Focus+1
Gladiator	Boxing+1
Infantry	Melee+1
Artillery	Ranged+1
Propagandist	Art+1
Cryptic	Languages+1
Geomancer	Science+1
Paladin	Parry+1
Champion	Strike+1

Ogres have the following Limit values:

ENCUMBRANCE: 1 + Body + Strength + Psychokinesis
MOVE/COMBAT: Body + Agility + Telepathy
MOVE/TRAVEL: Body + Agility + Clairvoyance

Ogres appear like superhumanly tall, brutish and primitive looking Humans, standing between nine and eleven feet tall. They have sharp, tusk-like teeth, and enjoy eating human-style foods more than any other race of Fairy. They are known to dine upon an unwary human traveler from time to time as well, but are careful not to over-hunt, saving us for special occasions.

Ogres are often depicted in human stories as savage and unthinking creatures, but that is more a matter of Human prejudice against Giants. Ogres are surprisingly sophisticated, every bit as civilized as Gnomes, they just lead more pastoral lives without all the gizmos and weird science. They can be quite brutal however, to the credit of those who tell such stories, for the Ogres are great lovers of war and its tools. They have a special knack for the use and deployment of artillery and siege weapons, and they are believed to have been originally created for the purpose of some ancient and forgotten war between Humans and Elves, but were never deployed, and dream about great conquests while living quiet working class lives.

Ogre females will only give birth once in their immortal lives, and always to twins. The father will be whichever male Ogre who mates with her first. It will take the mother 18 month to carry the twins to term, and it will take them twice as long as a Human child to reach adulthood.

Ogres prefer living on highland steppes, in mountain valleys, rocky hill country, and on mesas and mountaintops. Most raise goats or sheep as livestock, but steppe dwelling Ogres will breed horses for their milk and meat. Ogres do not like cows and bulls, and will try to avoid them.

Ogres spend the least amount of time underground of all the Fairy Folk, some living entirely within above-ground buildings and fortresses, often the ruins of abandoned human structures. The Barrows they construct are huge, but are used for official business and ceremonies, and for the storage of goods to keep their community fed during the winter months. Only mountain-dwelling Ogres are known to build their dwellings underground, in Caverns they deem large enough.

The Ogre's great size and natural strength make them able to carry Oversized items as if they were normal items, and make use of Giant Sized Items.

Ogres Shrug damage to their Health Status with an Average Body + Focus action, to reduce damage taken since their Turn by 1/2 (rounding down, minimum 0).

Ogres receive a bonus 1D6 to dice pools when making Perception actions that involve their sense of smell.

Ogres have a Bite Attack that they can make on a successfully grappled opponent, with no roll to hit, that does an amount of Health damage equal to the Ogres' Body Score.

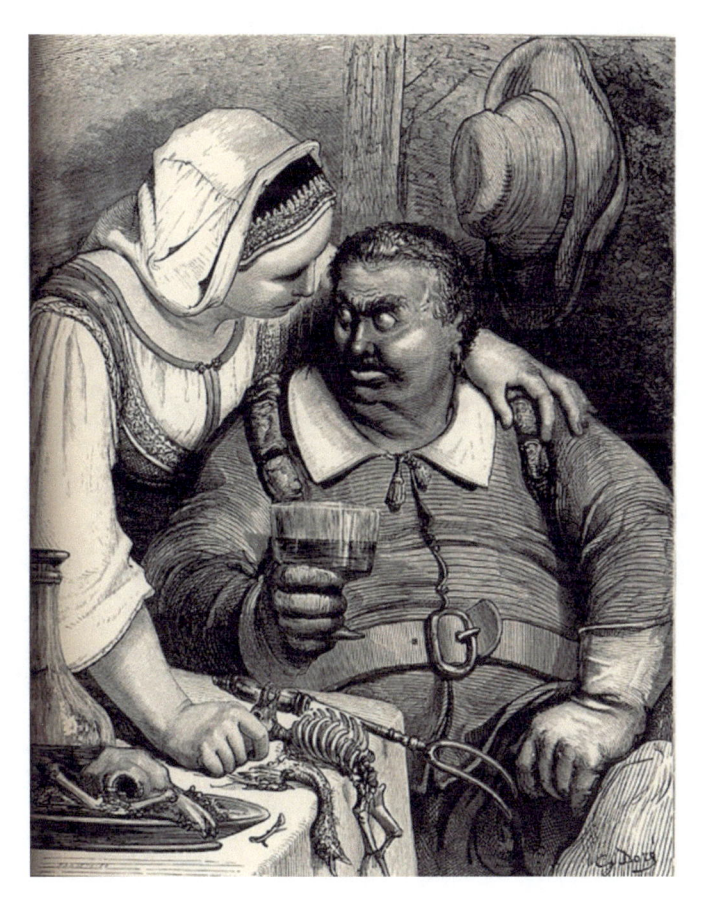

STARTING COINS: Body x100 (Silver)

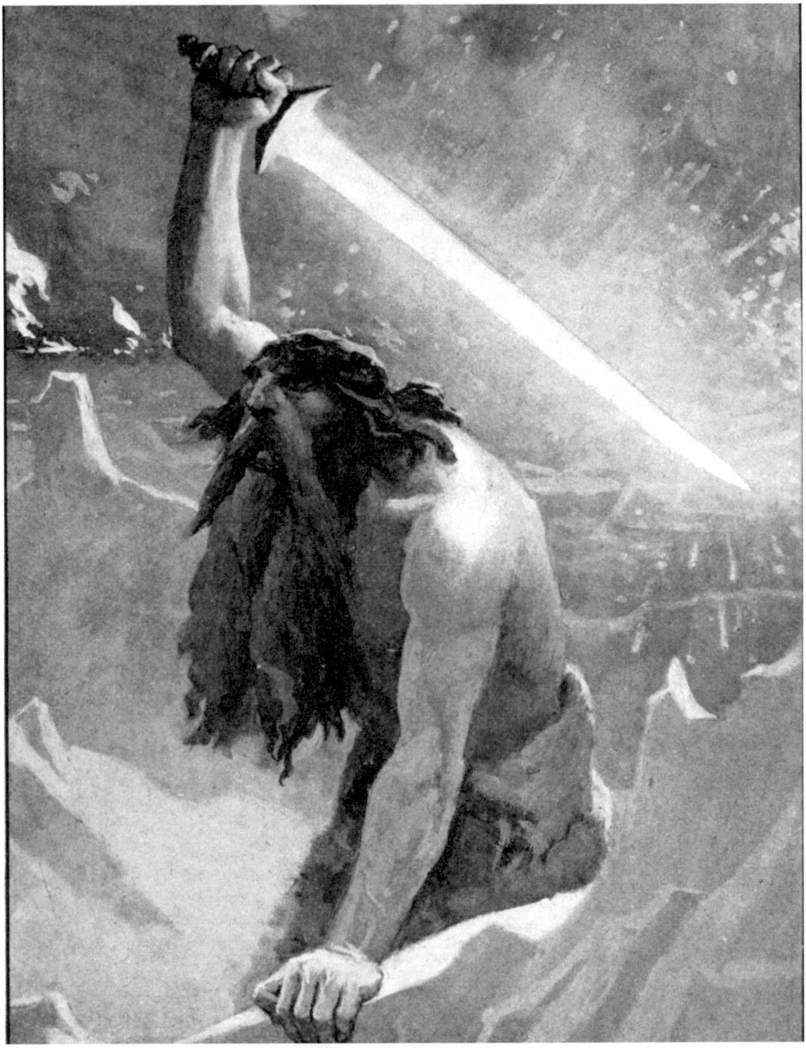

Giant Items

Ogres will begin the game with 3 items selected from either Commoner or Giant Item equipment options. They rely on trade with Gnomes for most of their manufactured goods, and those who cannot afford clothes big enough to fit them, will often wear rags tied into a simple loincloth for modesty's sake.

Giant Items count as Oversized items if carried by Humans and smaller Inhumans. Their Weapons cannot be used in combat, and Giant Armor and Clothing grants no benefits from being worn by anything smaller than an Ogre, only partial cover.

GIANT CLOTHES
Giant Peasant Outfit
Giant Dress
Giant Boots
Giant Hat

GIANT ARMOR	DEFENSE	DETAILS
Giant Winter Coat	Padded	
Giant Leather Armor	Plated	
Giant Half-Plate	Plated	
Giant Helmet		Full Suit with Leather or Half-Plate
Giant Shield		+3 Dodge/Parry

GIANT WEAPONS	DAMAGE	RANGE
Throwing Boulder	4	2
Cannonball (thrown)	3	3
Giant Club	3	close
Giant Knife	3	close
Giant Spear	4	3
Giant Sword	4	close
Giant Ax	5	close
Giant Crossbow	5	
Giant Bomb	5 to range 4	3
Giant Net	Hard to escape	2

GIANT EQUIPMENT	DETAILS
Quiver of Giant Bolts	3 Giant Crossbow Bolts
Giant Torch	burns for 2 hours
Giant Camping Kit	start campfire + blanket
Giant Tool Kit	+1 structure construction
Giant Jewelry	+1 Beauty
Giant Backpack	+4 Encumbrance

LIVESTOCK
Goat/Sheep
Boar
Horse
Cat

112

Fairy Magic

Fairy Folk who are skilled in Divine or Occult magic differ from mortal humans in how they make use of it. Though they may have a physical form, Fairy Folk are still more closely related to spirits than to beings of flesh and blood, and like spirits and ghosts, they do not need to make use of pre-crafted spells for Occult skills. The powers of Divine skills are largely unchanged, but any failure during a Prayer or Exorcism ritual will shatter any form of disguise they may be using, to reveal their true form for all to see. This will end the effects of Metamorphosis and Illusions immediately, upon any failed Divine action. Physical costumes and disguises being worn by the Fairy will suddenly appear obviously fraudulent.

The Fairy use of Occult magic is even more dramatically different. Fairies do not need to craft and memorize spells. They can attempt any possible spell effect for the Occult skills they have points in, at the difficulty a mortal spellcaster attempting to craft that spell would have to overcome. Spell effects are generally measured by how severely they alter reality or something's natural state. They can be rated as Minor, Significant, or Major in their power level. Fairy Magic can be permanent if the spell being replicated would have been, but any living being or object that has been effected by a Fairy's magic will see the effect end if they enter an area marked as Holy Ground, and revert to normal.

Fairy Magic is +2 to the difficulty if the Fairy tries to cast an effect on themselves, and they cannot use magic at all if on Holy Ground. Demonology effects directed towards other Fairy Folk are +4 to their difficulty. A Fairy cannot summon itself, intentionally or by accident.

The Severity of a Spell effect is determined by how difficult that spell is to craft. The difficulties of the different levels of Severity are as follows:

SEVERITY	DIFFICULTY
Minor	Hard
Significant	Very hard
Major	Impossible

Fairy Folk may cast a number of spell effects or Divine Prayers equal to their Spirit + Focus, before they will require at least 4 hours of sleep to replenish their energies and use Occult magic again. They do not have a separate Daily Prayer limit like a Human with Divine Skills, all of a Fairy's magic is fueled from the same source.

MAGIC LIMIT: Spirit + Focus

Fairies who employ Metamorphosis to appear human, or to have a human size, will loose all benefits they normally gain from being Tiny or Giant. Pixies grown to human proportions while retaining their winged form will only be able to continue to fly at that size with a MOVE/ FLIGHT Limit equal to their Psychokinesis skill.

Fairy Changelings

There are many creatures in legend that have been called changelings at one time or another, but the most famous of all are those of Fairy origin.

As spiritual beings, Fairies not only use Occult magic like ghosts and spirits, but they can also possess the minds of mortals and wear their bodies as if they were their own. The mortal must have both their Sanity and Morale Incapacitated, and they must be within the line of sight of the Fairy attempting possession. The Fairy will first make a Hard Mind+Telepathy action to invade the mortal's thoughts and override their self-control, followed by a Very difficult Body + Psychokinesis action to turn themselves into psychic energy, appearing as a floating light that then enters the chest of their target. If both rolls are successful, the Fairy takes full control over the mortal body, replacing their Mind and Spirit Attributes, Sanity and Morale Statuses, and Skills with their own, keeping only the host's Body Score.

The Fairy can make a Hard Mind+Telepathy action to look for specific memories the host has, and is in complete control over them for as long as they wish to remain in their body. The Fairy can leave their host at any time they choose, and will teleport to the nearest Fairy Circle to reappear in their own form. They will be forced to leave if their host body is killed, if either of their own Sanity or Morale Statuses become Incapacitated, if they enter Holy Ground, or a successful Exorcism ritual is performed upon them.

Both Goblins and Church Pixies are especially prone to engaging in this sort of behavior, as it allows them to travel around a Human settlement incognito, and with a little Telepathic effort to assume their host' identity and life. People who know them best will be able to tell that something is different, and if the Fairy is not careful, they could draw the attention of Church Exorcists down upon themselves. If they can hold onto their host, they can live out whole lives. Taste foods, get drunk. Have sex. Raise children. Grow old and die. And still have eternity to be themselves again after.

Fairy Death

Fairy Folk are ageless, immortal beings, who always seem to return after you think they've been destroyed. But it is possible to kill one permanently, if one goes about things in the correct sequence of events. First, the Fairy must have its Sanity Incapacitated. It will rant and rave for a Turn before Teleporting away to recover for the next 28 days. If its Morale is then damaged before its next Turn comes around, while it is still having some form of crazed ranting fit, the teleportation will be delayed. If its Morale is then further attacked until Incapacitated, giving the Fairy no time to get away, it will still delay teleportation. At this point, with both its Morale and Sanity at 0, Incapacitating its Health will kill the Fairy. It will turn into a white stony substance as if it were a statue of itself, which will crumble away to dust after 28 days. If at any point the Fairy is able to get away from its attacker, or be left alone, for at least 3 minutes it will teleport away and recover like normal.

FAIRY FOLK

Name: Level:
Role: Primary Skills:
Talent: Occupation:

ATTRIBUTES/STATUS

BODY   HEALTH

MIND   SANITY

SPIRIT   MORALE

SKILLS

BODY
Agility
Beauty
Strength

MIND
Knowledge
Perception
Technology

SPIRIT
Charisma
Empathy
Focus

COMBAT
Boxing
Melee
Ranged

STRANGE
Art
Languages
Science

MARTIAL
Dodge
Parry
Strike

PSIONICS
Clairvoyance
Psychokinesis
Telepathy

DIVINE
Blessing
Exorcism
Healing

OCCULT
Demonology
Metamorphosis
Necromancy

LIMITS

ENCUMBRANCE: MAGIC LIMIT:
MOVE/COMBAT:
MOVE/TRAVEL:
MOVE/OTHER:

ITEMS

Armor: Weapon:
Other:
Spells:
Special Abilities: XP:

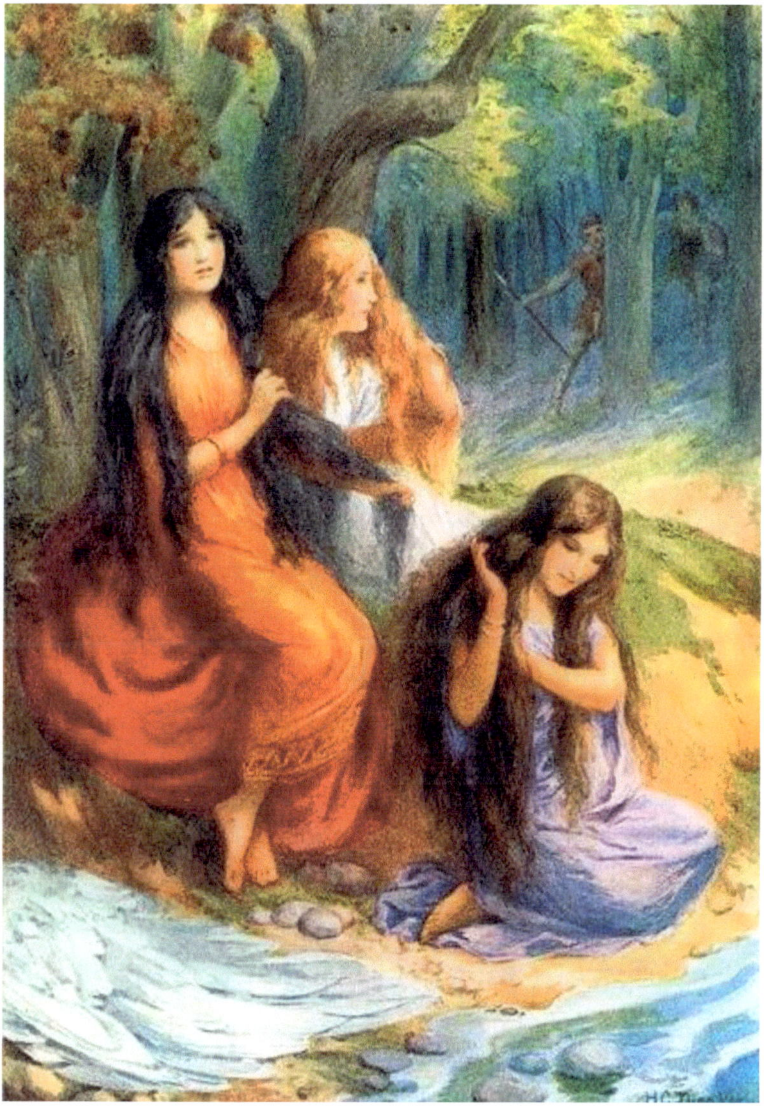

Fairy Friends

"Fairy Friends" is a way of describing an assortment of Inhuman races which are civilized enough to interact with both Fairy and Human societies, and are not Shapeshifters. Most Fairy Friends are mortal beings of flesh and bone, but at least one of their number are spirits who have taken physical form in imitation of the Fairy Folk.

Each race of Fairy Friend has its own special abilities and culture. They may live and work alongside Fairies, (and Humans on occasion), but they are distinct unto themselves, and may have communities of their own away from both Fairy and Human settlements.

Like Fairies, each race of Fairy Friend serves as a Character's Role, with a Primary school of skills. Starting level Fairy Friend Characters receive 5 points to add to skills in that category. No Primary skill may be raised higher than +4 with points during Character Creation.

Once the Role's Primary category has had points placed in its skills, the Player will then select their Fairy Friend's Lineage, a sub-culture, tribe, or ethnicity within the Fairy Friend's race that grants them a Sub-Class, and a second school of Primary skills. They will receive 3 points for skills in the Lineage's primary school, with the same restrictions for all primary skills.

Once points have been added to skills in both of their Character's Primary categories, they will then select an Occupation. Their Occupation will determine a specific skill they receive an additional +1 bonus to, even if this raises a skill as high as +5.

The Character then receives a final 3 points to add to skills in their primary categories, to their Occupational skill, or to any skill in the schools of Body, Mind, Spirit, Combat, and Strange. No skill outside of their primary categories may be higher than +3. Like most Humans and Fairies, Fairy Friends are illiterate unless points have been placed in the Languages skill, or if the Role's text says otherwise.

Fairy Friends have both a Social Class, and a Sub-Class. Their primary Class is how all members of their race are generally considered to fit into the social hierarchy. Their Sub-Class indicates how their Lineage fits within their own unique culture, or how outsiders familiar with their Lineages may rank them separately from their kind as a whole.

INHUMANS	SKILLS	CLASS	PAGE
Satyr	Occult	Outlaw	125
Mermaid	Psionics	Nobility	136
Centaur	Body	Commoner	144
Cherub	Divine	Church	151
Swan Maiden	Martial	Nobility	159

SATYR

Lecherous Philosophers or Hedonistic Artists? Satyrs lure mortal women and men to join them in their wilderness revels.

CLASS: Outlaw
PRIMARY SKILLS: Occult

LINEAGE	SKILLS	SUB-CLASS
Faun	Divine	Outlaw
Devil	Psionics	Nobility
Succubus	Body	Commoner

Satyrs have the following Limits:

ENCUMBRANCE: 3 + Body + Strength
MOVE/COMBAT: 2 + Body + Agility
MOVE/TRAVEL: 4 + Body + Strength
MOVE/LEAP: Body + Strength

FAUN STARTING COINS: Spirit + Knowledge (Copper)
DEVIL STARTING COINS: Mind + Charisma (Silver)
SUCCUBUS STARTING COINS: Body + Beauty (Gold)

FAUN OCCUPATIONS	BONUS
Snatcher	Strength+1
Watcher	Perception+1
Listener	Empathy+1
Stalker	Ranged+1
Herbalist	Science+1
Runner	Dodge+1
Prophet	Clairvoyance+1
Druid	Blessing+1
Illusionist	Demonology+1

DEVIL OCCUPATIONS	BONUS
Butler	Agility+1
Mechanic	Technology+1
Mastermind	Focus+1
Coach	Boxing+1
Critic	Art+1
Entrepreneur	Strike+1
Mime	Psychokinesis+1
Whistler	Exorcism+1
Preacher	Necromancy+1

SUCCUBUS OCCUPATIONS	BONUS
Dancer	Beauty+1
Mistress	Knowledge+1
Conniver	Charisma+1
Escort	Melee+1
Secretary	Languages+1
Duelist	Parry+1
Dominatrix	Telepathy+1
Masseuse	Healing+1
Artist	Metamorphosis+1

Frequently mistaken for Fairy Folk, Satyrs are a long-lived but very mortal race of half-human goat people, who live in deep woodlands and mountainous highlands, where Humans fear to climb. The same exact types of places where Fairies like to build their own settlements.

The majority of Satyrs have no homes, and spend their time camping outdoors, either singly or in groups. Some will seek shelter in shallow caves when the weather is particularly bad, but only the Succubi are known to build shelters and live in one place for any length of time, and they never build anything more sophisticated than a straw hut or wooden shack. Satyrs of all Lineages get along with one another, and will get together and form large parties that may last for an entire season before breaking up to go their separate ways again. They are as a rule self-indulgent and at best only borderline narcissistic. They prioritize pleasure over duty, and are known for being unexpectedly rude if they think they can get a laugh at someone else's expense. Other Satyrs ignore such behavior among their peers, but Humans, Fairies, and even other Inhumans can find their company intolerable at times, considering them to be incapable of practicing good etiquette and manners.

They also have a poor grasp of personal boundaries and appropriate behavior. They can be sexually aggressive, which over time has led to their current status as Outlaws in most civilized places, both Human and Fairy.

FAUNS were once considered equals with Witches and Wild Pixies, as keepers of the Old Ways and protectors of sacred places, but they seduced one too many Priestesses, spoiled one too many ceremonies by sleeping with the Virgin Sacrifice, and now they conduct their ceremonies with mere handfuls of peasant maidens, in secret.

DEVILS are the most organized and rational of the Satyr Lineages, and thanks to their connections to the Nobility in both Human and Fairy Kingdoms, they were able to maintain their pedigree after the Fauns got all Satyrs branded as Outlaws. Devils can enter Fairy Cities freely, but those who have business with Humans must use stealth or disguise when walking among them.

SUCCUBI are what the Church calls Satyr women, who have been able to evade their Outlaw status in Human lands now that the Commoners think they are something different from the other Satyrs. Though they must avoid detection by the Church, who think they are devils, there are many a man in Human society who will gladly turn a blind eye to their presence.

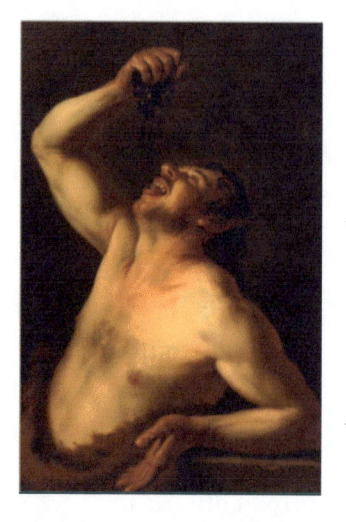

Satyrs appear as healthy and strangely attractive bipeds whose upper body from the waist up looks like that of a human, with goat or ram's horns growing out of their foreheads. From the waist down, they are covered with fur, and have legs like that of a goat, with hooves for feet. They are "romantically compatible" with both humans, and human-sized Fairies and other similar Inhumans, but are a unique species of life and can only breed with other Satyrs of the appropriate sex. They grow and develop at roughly the same pace as Humans, but once they reach adulthood, they can potentially live for over half a millennia, before old age creeps up on them. They will typically only have children once or twice a century. Satyrs do not form stable mated pairings. Their Kids are usually raised by their mother, although some will foist them on their father if they think them too much trouble.

Satyrs need to eat, drink, and sleep in much the same quantities as Humans require to survive. They can be injured and die, and they are susceptible to disease and illness. Satyr eyesight and hearing is on par with a Human's, but their senses of taste, smell, and touch are actually slightly muted compared to what Humans experience, which is in part why they are so instinctively driven to overindulge themselves. They eat large meals or engage in hours of lovemaking at a time because they are trying to taste or feel it.

Satyrs are more superhuman than supernatural. Their cultural practice of occultism differs little from the Occult skills and spells Humans use. Their only special abilities are their naturally athletic physiques, and the benefits granted by the goat-like parts of their anatomy:

Male Satyrs have horns that give them Plated armor defense against Boxing and Melee attacks if they can see their opponent. They can also use them to make a head-butting Boxing attack that inflicts 3 levels of Health damage.

Female Satyrs have smaller horns that give them Plated armor defense against Boxing attacks if they can see their opponent, and inflict 1 level of Health damage with a Boxing attack to head-butt.

All Satyrs can climb anything at Easy difficulty if the surface gives them anything that they can gain even the slightest purchase with using their hooves, unless the surface is upside down or tilted into an overhang. They can Leap from purchase to purchase from a stand-still at half their normal MOVE/LEAP Limit (rounded up).

With a brief running start, a Satyr can Leap incredible distances as determined in 10-foot spaces by their MOVE/LEAP Limit. Leaping from a standing position, or attempting to Leap straight-up, reduces their Leap Limit by half (rounded up).

The native Language of Satyrs is music, and they can add both of their skill bonuses from Art and Languages to Spirit actions using music to communicate feelings and ideas, or for pure entertainment. Satyrs have learned to speak normally when talking to Humans, Fairies, and other Inhumans.

Satyrs can use the vast majority of Human and Fairy made objects, with the exceptions of pants, hosiery, and other types of clothing designed for human-type legs. A Satyr will require a long dress, gown, or robes to conceal their goat-like lower body. Satyrs cannot wear boots, shoes, sandals, or any other type of footwear. Most Satyrs are casual nudists anyway, but some have taken to wearing the articles of human clothing that will fit on their torsos and arms.

Satyrs recover lost Status in the same manner and pacing as Humans, but they will often employ magical means to speed up the process when they can. Devils and Succubi are both also fond of using Metamorphosis spells on themselves in order to take on a completely Human form, but their Faun kin think poorly of forming a habit out of it, and will only do so briefly, mostly when they are recruiting new girls to join their woodland cults.

Satyrs who take on human form loose both their Horn attack/defense, and their Move/Leap.

FAUNS will begin the game with a musical instrument of their choice from the Satyr options, and 3 items of choice from the Commoner equipment options, including clothing items.

DEVILS start off with the upper half of a suit of the style worn by Lords or Wizards, with a Nice Hat. They will have a musical instrument from the Satyr options, and may also select 2 items from the Commoner, Noble, and Church equipment options.

SUCCUBI begin the game with a Peasant Dress, a musical instrument from the Satyr options, and Jewelry. They will also select 2 items from the Commoner equipment options.

SATYR INSTRUMENTS
Pan Pipes
Fiddle
Hand Cymbals
Maracas
Mandolin
Harmonica
Bagpipe
Accordion

SATYR EQUIPMENT	Details
Instrument Case	Hold instrument and pocket items
Stage Kit	+1 Stage Performance
Massage Oil Bottle	5 Doses, +1 Seduction attacks

MERMAID

The beloved daughters of the Sea Gods, the beautiful Mermaids lure sailors and beachcombers to their doom, in order to continue their Noble line of inheritance.

CLASS: Nobility
PRIMARY SKILLS: Psionics

LINEAGE	SKILLS	SUB-CLASS
Fish Maiden	Divine	Commoner
Sea Hag	Occult	Outlaw
Royal	Strange	Nobility

Mermaids have the following Limits:

ENCUMBRANCE: = Strength
MOVE/COMBAT: 1+ Agility
MOVE/TRAVEL: 1 + Strength
MOVE/SWIM: 2 + Body + Agility

STARTING PEARLS: 10 + Spirit + Beauty

Mermaids are half-human, half-fish women who are believed to be the mortal descendants of ancient gods of the sea, your Poseidons and Neptunes and such, who mated with mortal women. Mermaids have existed ever since as they are now, seemingly unchanging while the surface world goes through constant shifts of whom is the Ruler, and the Ruled. They only give birth to Mermaids. If there are such a thing as Mermen, I've never heard tale of it. Mermaids must rely on capturing sailors, fishermen, and any Human male who walks too close to the shoreline where they are hunting. They will be seduced, and then drowned in the aftermath of their love-play.

Mermaids age at the same rate as Humans, but can only recover their Status when submerged in seawater for the required amount of time to heal. When submerged in seawater they recover lost Status levels in half the time it takes Humans to recover the same amount of damage. They can breathe in freshwater if they need to, but will not be able to recover Status until they are back in a saltwater environment.

Mermaids can breathe both air and water, and require some of both every day. They can remain out of the water, breathing air only, for a number of hours equal to their Body Score, before they must go back underwater for at least an hour before coming back up. Reducing the time spent above the surface reduces the time needed before they can come back up for their full Breath Limit. Mermaids breathe water magically without use of gills. They must come up to the surface to breathe air for at least five minutes per 24 hour period, to keep their lungs healthy.

Mermaids cannot talk when underwater, and must rely on sign language and telepathy to communicate with one another.

Mermaids appear as human women from the waist up. From the waist down they are covered in colorful fish scales, and their feet are broad and webbed to form paddle-like fins. They still possess two legs, not a singular fish tail in place of them, but if viewed in the correct pose or from certain angles, it is easy to see how people got the impression that they had tails and no feet.

FISH MAIDENS are the Commoners of Mermaid Society, and like to live near the coast, especially around rocky shorelines.

FISH MAIDEN OCCUPATION	BONUS
Surfer	Agility+1
Lifeguard	Perception+1
Flirt	Charisma+1
Drown Maiden	Boxing+1
Seamstress	Art+1
Skirmisher	Parry+1
Cassandra	Clairvoyance+1
Healer	Healing+1
Fish Wife	Metamorphosis+1

SEA HAGS are Mermaid witches, who typically live by themselves or in small covens, around isolated islands far from mainland shores.

SEA HAG OCCUPATIONS	BONUS
Pearl Diver	Strength+1
Scavenger	Knowledge+1
Conspirator	Focus+1
Butcher	Melee+1
Oceanographer	Science+1
Shark Maiden	Strike+1
Sea Witch	Psychokinesis+1
Sea Priestess	Exorcism+1
Cold Fish	Necromancer+1

ROYAL Mermaids live in castles made of coral, on reefs found in the open ocean, far from land or island. They travel frequently, to find Noble men worthy of their attentions.

ROYAL OCCUPATIONS
Sunbather
Salvager
Ambassador
Harpooner
Bookworm
Officer
Mesmerizer
Politician

BONUS
Beauty+1
Technology+1
Empathy+1
Ranged+1
Languages+1
Dodge+1
Telepathy+1
Demonology+1

Mermaids have restrictions on the types of garments they can wear in much the same way as Satyrs, however they can wear pants if they can fit their feet through them. The cannot wear shoes and footwear of any kind, and must rely on dresses to hide their feet. They are by nature nudists in their natural form, but know that Humans and many

Fairies can be uncomfortable about such displays of skin, and so Mermaids have adopted the use of shells and strings of pearls to make rudimentary bras. They can also wear articles of human clothing that would fit on their torsos or heads. They can only wear dresses and outfits with pants if they are out of the water, otherwise they find them too restrictive for swimming.

When on land, or aboard a boat or ship, their feet can be used to Move/Combat or Travel, but at the low rates as indicated by those Limit Values. All movement underwater, both in Combat or distance Travel, uses their Move/Swimming Limit.

All Mermaid Characters start their adventures with a Purse, a small bag with a strap that allows them to carry a few more items (3), and numerous pocket sized items, without need of holding them in their hands, or securing them to a belt. They may also select 2 items from the Mermaid Equipment options below:

MERMAID CLOTHING	DETAILS
Modesty Jewelry	+1 Beauty
Gossamer Veil	+1 Beauty
Seashell Jewelry	+1 Charisma
Pearl Necklace	+1 Beauty
Belt	secures up to 3 Pouches
Back Harness	secures 1 basket or 2 items

ARMOR	DEFENSE	DETAILS
Sharkskin	Padded	+1 Charisma
Baleen Plate	Plated	
Coral Helmet	Full Suit with Sharkskin or Baleen Plate	

WEAPONS	DAMAGE	RANGE
Knife	1	close
Short-Spear	2	1
Trident	3	close
Harpoon	3	2
Net	Hard to escape	2

EQUIPMENT	DETAILS
Basket	+3 Encumbrance
Belt Pouch	+1 Encumbrance
Salvaged Scrap	Commoner Item

CENTAUR

Dwellers of hidden meadowlands, deserts, and plains, Centaurs are a simple people who will cross paths, and spears, with both Fairy and Man.

CLASS: Commoner
PRIMARY SKILLS: Body

LINEAGE	SKILLS	SUB-CLASS
Barbarian	Combat	Outlaw
Nomad	Strange	Church
Shepherd	Spirit	Commoner

Centaurs use the following Limit values:

ENCUMBRANCE: 4 + Body + Strength
MOVE/COMBAT: 3 + Body + Agility
MOVE/TRAVEL: 5 + Body + Strength
MOVE/INDOORS: 1 + Agility

BARBARIAN STARTING COINS: Body + Strength (Gold)
NOMAD STARTING COINS: 10 + Mind + Charisma (Silver)
SHEPHERD STARTING COINS: Spirit x10 (Copper)

Centaurs are a mortal species of half-human, half-horses, that look human from the waist up, but from the waist down they have the full four-legged body and tail of a horse, starting at what would have been a normal horse's neckline. Their height, weight, and unusual shape prevent them from reaching certain areas, especially if climbing is involved. Trees, ladders, ropes, and steep inclines are always at least Impossible difficulty for them to climb. Only broad steps and trails along ledges leading upward are accessible to Centaurs. They are also often too large to fit through many doors, and find being inside buildings and underground spaces to be too confining, unless a massive amount of open floorspace is available to them, such as in an arena.

Centaurs are terrible swimmers, with a swimming Move speed of 1, instead of at half of their normal Move/Travel Limit as it is for Humans.

The Centaur's unique body shape allows them to not only carry the amount of items as determined by their Encumbrance Limit, but to also potentially carry a number of human-sized riders (seated on their horsebacks) equal to their Body Score -1 (minimum 0). If they are not carrying any riders, they can instead be harnessed to pull a cart, or a wagon alongside a horse or another Centaur. They can also wear saddlebags in addition to having a backpack on their torso.

Centaurs take twice as long to gestate in the womb, but otherwise age, live, reproduce, recover, and die at the same pace as Humans. They have no supernatural abilities, and few among them elect to learn magical skills or any sort, though nothing prevents them from doing so if they wish, with the lone exception of Psionics, which they have no latent talent for whatsoever.

BARBARIAN Centaurs live by no one's rules but their own, out on the open meadowlands and mixed wilderness reaches, often in between the territories of Humans and Fairy Folk. They are proud raiders and excellent field infantry.

BARBARIAN OCCUPATIONS	BONUS
Athlete	Strength+1
Ranger	Perception+1
Chief	Charisma+1
Warrior	Melee+1
Crafter	Art+1
Berserker	Strike+1
Druid	Blessing+1
Shaman	Demonology

NOMAD Centaurs travel around and between desert lands, and are devoted to their own version of the Human Church. They are proficient traders, scouts, and couriers, with contacts in many settlements on the deserts' borders.

NOMAD OCCUPATIONS	BONUS
Sprinter	Agility+1
Trader	Technology+1
Outsider	Empathy+1
Cavalry	Ranged+1
Pilgrim	Languages+1
Messenger	Dodge+1
Channeler	Exorcism+1
Witchdoctor	Necromancy+1

SHEPHERD Centaurs live closest to Human settlements, and are considered the most civilized of them all, tending to herds of horse, cattle, sheep, pigs, goats, and even deer and buffalo.

SHEPHERD OCCUPATIONS	BONUS
Prancer	Beauty+1
Sage	Knowledge+1
Lookout	Focus+1
Wrestler	Boxing+1
Naturalist	Science+1
Protector	Parry+1
Healer	Healing+1
Magi	Metamorphosis

Centaurs can Shrug damage to their Health Status with an Average difficulty Body + Focus action on their next Turn following losing Status levels.

Centaurs can make a Stomp attack (Boxing) with their front hooves, which inflicts a number of levels of Health damage equal to their Body Score. A Stomp attack can only be used against a prone target. Their rear legs can deliver a powerful kick to targets located behind them, doing 3 levels of Health damage.

Centaurs can make a Charge attack to knock down a human sized or smaller target with a successful Boxing attack. If hit, the target will be stunned and knocked prone on the ground for a number of Turns equal to the Centaur's Strength skill bonus. If the Centaur has no points in Strength, the target is pushed aside, but remains standing.

Centaurs have the same restrictions on wearing human clothing as Satyrs do, only able to wear articles of clothing that can fit on their upper bodies alone. It is Apocalyptically difficult (Impossible+6) to conceal a Centaur's true nature without the aid of magic.

Centaurs begin their adventuring with either a Spear and a Net, or a Bow and a Quiver of Arrows. They may select 2 other items from Commoner or Centaur equipment options.

EQUIPMENT	DETAILS
Saddlebag	+2 Encumbrance
Saddle	holds 1 passenger
Horseshoes	+2 Move/Travel
Horse Armor	Plated

CHERUB

Friendly but mischievous Lesser Angels, Cherubs are Invisible benefactors of unsuspecting mortals.

CLASS: Church
PRIMARY SKILLS: Divine

LINEAGE	SKILLS	SUB-CLASS
Cupid	Psionics	Church
Gremlin	Mind	Outlaw
Imp	Occult	Church

Cherubs use the following Limit values:

ENCUMBRANCE: 1 + Strength
MOVE/COMBAT: 1 + Body + Agility + Clairvoyance
MOVE/TRAVEL: Body + Focus
MOVE/FLIGHT: Spirit + Psychokinesis

Cherubs have little need of money or equipment, rarely keeping Coins or Items. They have no Starting Coins or Items of equipment.

Cherubs are a race of spirits who dwell upon the same levels of the Heavens that the Fairy Folk originally came from, known by various names such as Avalon, Arcadia, Olympia, Eden, Paradise, and so on. They have long been friends of the Fairy, and after many thousands of years watching the Fairy Folk walk among mortals in the living world, some Cherubs gathered together and put their minds to it, to figure out a way to replicate what the Fairies had done so long ago.

They came close to success, but not entirely. Cherubs have physical bodies, made of a similar form of psychic matter as Fairy Folk, but if they ever have any of their Statuses Critically Injured, their body will turn into a pink granite stone, and their spirit-form will be banished back to the Heavens for a thousand years. They can only recover lost Status by spending an amount of time on Holy Ground as it would take a mortal to recover from a similar amount of damage, to any type of Status.

Cherubs look like human children, and stand between 3 and 4 feet tall, with undersized vestigial wings on their backs, which should be too small to allow them to fly, and yet they seem to do so out of an act of sheer willpower. The Cupid and Imp Lineages have feathered wings, and the Gremlins have wings that look like those of a bat. They can only reach a top speed of miles per hour equal to their Mind Score.

They neither require food or drink or slumber, and they are incapable of dreaming. They are on the other hand quite comfortable in buildings and spaces marked as Holy Ground by the Church, unlike their old Fairy neighbors.

Cherubs are naturally invisible, and can only be seen by Ghosts and Spirits in Astral Space, other Cherubs, Fairies and Shapeshifters, and Wizards and Witches. Mortals who have skill in Clairvoyance, Exorcism, Demonology, or Necromancy can also see them even if they are not technically a Wizard or Witch.

To everyone else they are completely invisible. They can still be heard, and touched, but are Very hard to detect with Perception unless they are making a lot of noise, such as talking. Combined with their short stature, Cherubs are Impossible difficulty to attack with Boxing or Melee attacks, and cannot be targeted with Ranged attacks at all. To those they are visible to, their small size makes them Hard to hit with an attack. Cherubs never wear armor, and seldom any other type of clothing either.

CUPIDS consider themselves to be the most devoted to spreading the Church's Good News, as Heralds for the Clergy, and as Guardian Angles over Church-members in good standing.

CUPID OCCUPATIONS	BONUS
Casanova	Beauty+1
Stalker	Perception+1
Admirer	Empathy+1
Archer	Ranged+1
Poet	Art+1
Inquisitor	Strike+1
Astrologer	Clairvoyance+1
Priest	Blessing+1
Diabolist	Demonology+1

GREMLINS are the least concerned with the affairs of saints and sinners, preferring to expand their understanding of Science and Technology. They are friendly to both Wizard and Gnome.

GREMLIN OCCUPATIONS	BONUS
Acrobat	Agility+1
Saboteur	Technology+1
Daredevil	Focus+1
Wrecker	Melee+1
Retroengineer	Science+1
Navigator	Dodge+1
Poltergeist	Psychokinesis+1
Fixer	Healing+1
Mad Scientist	Metamorphosis+1

IMPS devote themselves to keeping an eye on the Church's stray flock, the sinners in the community who could use a helping hand to get themselves back on track to the Good Life.

IMP OCCUPATIONS	BONUS
Enforcer	Strength+1
Bookie	Knowledge+1
Negotiator	Charisma+1
Bodyguard	Boxing+1
Envoy	Languages+1
Blackguard	Parry+1
Snitch	Telepathy+1
Witchfinder	Exorcism+1
Reaper	Necromancy+1

Though they need to go to Holy Ground if they need to recover, many Cherubs dwell in Fairy Cities, especially if they are aboveground. There are numerous ways that living among people who can see you is superior to being invisible. Cherubs are also able to possess mortals whose Sanity and Morale are Incapacitated in the same fashion as Fairy Folk do, if the Cherub has the requisite skills in Psionics to do so. Many will do this to make living in Human settlements easier for them. They can be forced out of the body in the same fashion as possessing Ghosts and other spirits.

Cherubs are not born nor created, they simply appear on occasion, and join up with others of their kind, once they have figured out how to turn their spiritual essence into psychic matter under their control. They appear as human children, but are eons old, and never age or grow up. They are effectively immortal for as long as they can avoid Incapacitation, and their subsequent banishment to the uppermost reaches of Heaven. The longer they exist in a physical form living among Humans and Fairies, the more modest they will become in their habit of wearing clothes, but their Invisibility among most Humans allows them to cling to their nudity. Those that spend most of their time in Fairy Cities are far more likely to wear clothing tailored for beings of their size.

Cherubs are not romantically active beings, although they do quite enjoy witnessing mortal love, and will encourage it when they see its potential. They are asexual and genderless. Some may look and identify as more male or female than others, but the differences are barely noticeable.

Cherubs of all Lineages are known for their great dislike of Satyrs, who share the sentiment. Satyrs who are able to see them will go to great lengths to thwart whatever agenda a Cherub they encounter may be up to. Cherubs meanwhile will gleefully undermine all of a Satyr's hard work putting together networks of contacts and cultists, just to spoil their sinful fun.

Cupids and Imps do take their beliefs in God and duties to the Church very seriously, which can be a bone of contention between them and the Fairies from time to time, as they are often blamed for the current state of the Garden Pixies. And yet Fairies are angels too, of a sort, and will not bar the Cherubs access to their Kingdoms.

SWAN MAIDEN

Lineages of women born with wings, Swan Maidens wield authority over the Kingdoms of both Fairy and Mortal.

CLASS: Nobility
PRIMARY SKILLS: Martial

LINEAGE	SKILLS	SUB-CLASS
Siren	Psionics	Commoner
Valkyrie	Divine	Nobility
Harpy	Occult	Outlaw

Swan Maidens have the following Limits:

ENCUMBRANCE: 1 + Body + Strength
MOVE/COMBAT: 1 + Body + Strength
MOVE/TRAVEL: Body + Strength
MOVE/FLIGHT: 5 + Body + Strength - (# of Items carried)

SIREN STARTING COINS: 10 + Body + Charisma (Gold)
VALKYRIE STARTING COINS: Spirit + Focus (Gold)
HARPY STARTING COINS: Mind x10 (Gold)

Swan Maidens are mortal human women whose maternal ancestors have all been born with feathered wings, resembling those of a swan, which become functional by the time the child reaches puberty. They are said to be the descendants of a powerful warrior goddess from the distant north, the first of the Valkyries: Judges, saviors, and executioners of mortals who have fallen in battle.

In time, those first generations of Valkyries grew in number, and spread into different populations who dwelled to the south of their frozen homelands. Sirens would arise among the Commoner Class, and soon after the first Harpies would be born to Swan Maidens who turned to witchcraft. But while only the Valkyries spoke with the sanction of the gods of war, their southern cousins were treated with all the same fear and respect from the Nobility of both Human and Fairy lands, as the Valkyries were due. It is widely believed that angering a Swan Maiden is bad luck for any nation, as it signals upcoming defeat in battle, which can lead to the crumbling of entire societies.

Swan Maidens have wingspans twice as wide as they stand tall, and can accelerate up to speeds of 50 miles per hour. Their wings give them Plated armor protection. Every number of years after the Swan Maiden reaches adulthood equal to their Body Score, they will need to completely shed their wings, which will happen while they are bathing in water deep enough to fully submerge themselves in. Their wings will take a number of months equal to their Body Score to regrow, and become functional again. During this period of regrowth, the Swan Maiden cannot fly or use their new wings for protection. This period is also the only time that Swan Maidens are able to become pregnant.

If the Swan Maiden is able to become pregnant while regrowing her wings, the new ones will fall back off, and they will not grow new wings until after the infant is weaned. Only then will their wings regrow. Their children are just as likely to be born as either gender as any other Human child, but only the girls will be born with wings. The male offspring of Swan Maidens are seemingly normal.

Swan Maidens cannot hover in place, and need to be in constant motion while flying or they will fall and take 1 level of Health damage per 10 feet fallen. They can attempt to Shrug Off this damage. If they fall more than 20 feet they may be able catch themselves with their wings and reestablish flight with a Hard Body + Agility action.

Swan Maidens need at least 50 feet of clearance in order to take off, and while below 50 feet in altitude, they may take no other action except to fly. Above 50 feet, they can coast for one Turn at a time between Move actions, at half their Move/Flight speed, to be able to make a different action, like using weapons or items.

Landing is not automatic, it requires a Mind + Agility action at Average difficulty. Failure means the Character crash lands, will start their next Turn prone on the ground, and will take 1 level of Health and 1 level of Morale damage. They may choose to use their next Turn to try to Shrug Off one of these two levels of damage down to zero.

Hiding their wings beneath any kind of restrictive clothing that covers or otherwise interferes with their wings negates their flying and protection benefits. Binding their wings on purpose will have the same effect. The wings can be targeted for attacks, instead of the Swan Maiden herself. Each wing has Plated armor defense, and has 3 Health levels. The Swan Maiden can try to Shrug Off damage to her wings. Each wing must be targeted separately, unless with an area effect weapon like a flamethrower. Wings recover at the same rate as the Swan Maiden's own Health Status, separately from their owner's Status recovery. If a wing is lowered to 0 Health levels, it becomes crippled, and will no longer be able to be used for flight or gliding until it is shed and regrown.

Swan Maidens have no other powers to speak of, save for the same forms of magic humans can learn to use. If not for their wings, and their limited windows of ovulation, they would be impossible to distinguish from other Human women.

SIRENS are Swan Maidens whose fathers were Commoners instead of Kings. They are the most numerous of their kind, and those most likely for a Human to meet, dwelling near ponds and lakes.

SIREN OCCUPATIONS	BONUS
Temptress	Beauty+1
Chronicler	Knowledge+1
Actress	Charisma+1
Sharpshooter	Ranged+1
Singer	Art+1
Messenger	Dodge+1
Sorceress	Psychokinesis+1
Nurse	Healing+1
Invoker	Demonology+1

VALKYRIES are Swan Maidens of noble birth and Title. They continue to train in the arts of war, like the fearsome Shield-Maidens of olden times, and mete out justice on the battlefield.

VALKYRIE OCCUPATIONS	BONUS
Ace	Agility+1
Engineer	Technology+1
Officer	Focus+1
Infantry	Melee+1
Philosopher	Science+1
Knight	Parry+1
Norn	Clairvoyance+1
Paladin	Blessing+1
Priestess	Necromancy+1

HARPIES are Swan Maidens who have turned to witchery and statecraft, marked by their black swan wings. They reject the ways of the Valkyries, and lurk in isolated lairs, weaving their plots.

HARPY OCCUPATIONS	BONUS
Kidnapper	Strength+1
Sentinel	Perception+1
Torturer	Empathy+1
Bushwhacker	Boxing+1
Recordkeeper	Languages+1
Huntress	Strike+1
Hypnotist	Telepathy+1
Banisher	Exorcism+1
Enchantress	Metamorphosis+1

Swan Maidens occupy a unique position that is above and outside of the twins societies of Fairies and Men. Of Old Ways and the Church. Most Human and Fairy authorities will act with deference to any Swan Maidens they may encounter. Even Harpies are given the red-carpet treatment by non-Swan Maidens who are not aware of what they do with the men they lure out to their lairs in the wilderness. Humans who have heard of harpies would believe them to be monstrous avian creatures who eat unwary travelers, never realizing that they and the black-winged Swan Maidens are one in the same. For now, they are Outcasts only among the other Swan Maiden Lineages. Valkyries, meanwhile, are seen as agents of God Almighty by the Church, considered to be angelic beings.

Swan maidens have little in the way of restrictions to the types of items, clothes, and armor they may possess, except that anything they wear on their torso must be tailored to give their wings sufficient mobility. Only heavy cloaks or robes are sufficient enough to attempt to hide their wings under, and even then, they will be Hard to conceal. In most other instances their wings are Impossible difficulty to conceal from even a casual inspection.

Sirens will begin their adventuring with a Peasant Dress, and 3 items of choice from the Commoner or Church equipment options.

Valkyries begin with a Nice Dress, a suit of Knight Plate armor, a Sword or Spear, and 2 additional items selected from the Commoner, Nobility, or Church equipment options.

Harpies start their adventures with a Dark Dress, a Grimoire, and 2 items of choice from the Commoner, Magician, or Outlaw options.

INHUMAN

Name: *Level:*
Role: *Primary Skills:*
Lineage: *Primary Skills:*
Occupation: *XP:*

ATTRIBUTES/STATUS

BODY HEALTH

MIND SANITY

SPIRIT MORALE

SKILLS

BODY *MIND* *SPIRIT*
Agility Knowledge Charisma
Beauty Perception Empathy
Strength Technology Focus

COMBAT *STRANGE* *MARTIAL*
Boxing Art Dodge
Melee Languages Parry
Ranged Science Strike

PSIONICS *DIVINE* *OCCULT*
Clairvoyance Blessing Demonology
Psychokinesis Exorcism Metamorphosis
Telepathy Healing Necromancy

LIMITS

ENCUMBRANCE: SPELL MEMORY:
MOVE/COMBAT: DAILY PRAYERS:
MOVE/TRAVEL: Special Abilities:
MOVE/OTHER:

ITEMS

Armor: Weapon:
Grimoire: Other:

169

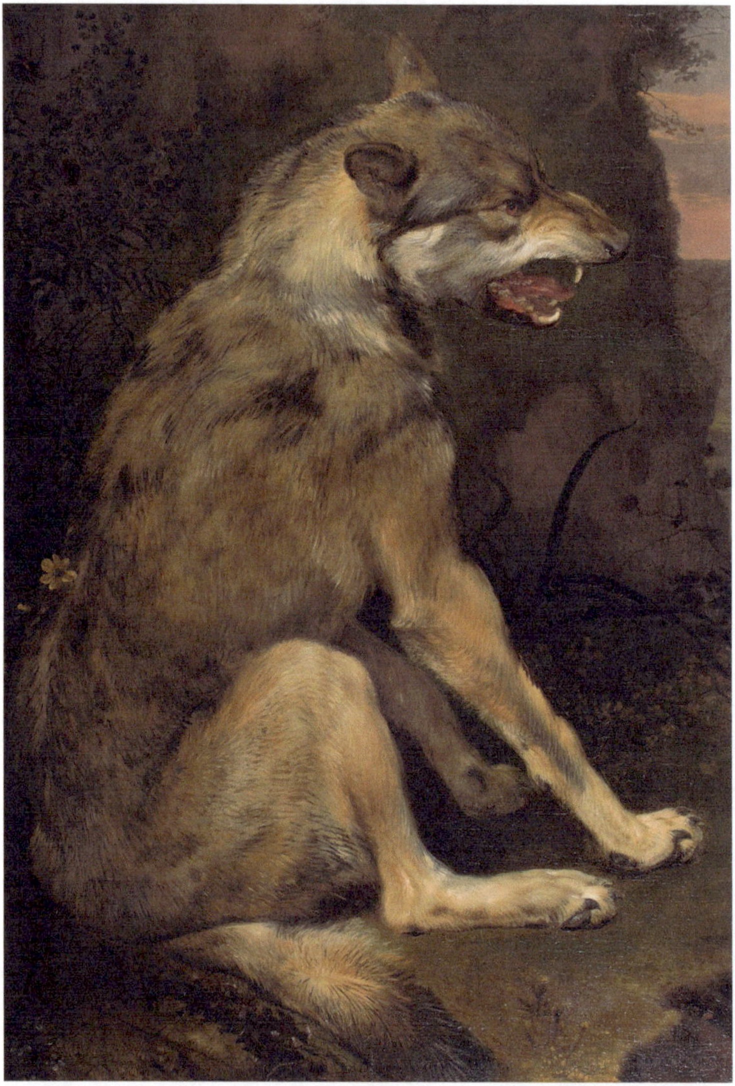

Shapeshifters

Shapeshifters are a loose association of mortal Humans who can change their form into that of an animal without need of using Metamorphosis spells, along with a couple of oddities such as the Pooka, who are mortal victims of Metamorphosis magic, or the Nymphs, who are the spiritual avatars of ancient psychic trees.

Shared experiences living between civilization and the natural world, and never being able to truly belong in either, keep the peace between different kinds of Shapeshifters and give them reason to associate with one another. There is no real Shapeshifter culture, however. Most are trying to live normal human lives, they are not trying to establish some sort of "third kingdom" alongside the reigning Humans and Fairies.

Many Shapeshifters dislike the Fairy Folk, the Pooka universally so, due to how they are created. Only Cat-Sith will ever be found living in Fairy communities, often remaining in cat form as much as possible.

Shapeshifters are also distinctly different from the other Inhumans collectively known as "Fairy Friends". They may also understand what it is like to not fit into either Human or Fairy society, but the Fairy Friends are more obviously Inhuman than Shapeshifters are (excepting the Pooka).

Shapeshifters are far more familiar with what Humans are really like, and what they really think of the other sentient peoples of the world when they are out of earshot, than any other form of Inhuman. All Shapeshifters, except (once again) the Pooka, are considered to be witches and outlaws by the Church, but there is little to no enforcement from the Nobility or Commoner authorities, unless Werewolves are involved.

Each Shapeshifter Species has its own unique abilities regarding their shapeshifting, and will determine which Human Class they build their Character with. Shapeshifters have the same number of Skill points and options of Roles and Occupations as Humans of the same Class.

SPECIES	CLASS	SKILLS	PAGE
Werewolf	Outlaw	Martial	174
Selkie	Church	Divine/Spirit	181
Nymph	Nobility	Strange	187
Pooka	Commoner	Body/Mind	195
Cat-Sith	Magician	Psionics/Occult	

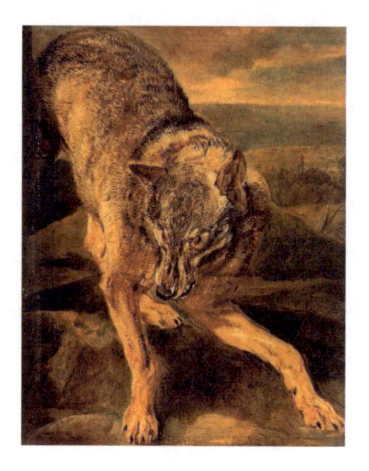

WEREWOLF

Cursed to take the form of a Wolf whenever they are exposed to moonlight.

CLASS: Outlaw

Werewolf Characters have the Role of Outlaw, and determine their Background, Skills, and Equipment with the same guidelines as Human Outlaw Characters.

Werewolves are Humans who are transformed into the form of a Wolf if they see the moon, or are directly exposed to moonlight.

It takes 1 Turn to shift forms, and all Status levels that have been damaged will be fully recovered by the time the transformation to wolf is complete.

Once in Wolf form, the Werewolf must succeed on a Hard Mind + Focus action to stay sentient and keep control of their Character for the duration of their time in wolf shape. If they fail, the wolf will be out of their control, and will act on instinct.

While in Wolf form, the Werewolf gains a Claw attack and a Bite attack, both of which inflict 2 levels of Health damage. They also gain a Howl attack (Spirit + Charisma) that inflicts 1 Morale damage to any who hear it, if the Werewolf using the Howl can beat their resistance.

In Wolf form, the Werewolf can Shrug off damage at Average difficulty. Their fur also gives them Padded armor defense.

The wolves' senses give the Werewolf a +2 bonus to Perception actions involving hearing or smell. They can also see clearly in low-light conditions. Their wolf form has the following Limits:

ENCUMBRANCE: = Strength
MOVE/COMBAT: 2 + Body + Agility
MOVE/TRAVEL: 4 + Body + Strength
MOVE/LEAP: = Strength

While in wolf form the Werewolf cannot speak, but will still understand written and spoken language if they remained in control of themselves after shapeshifting. Actions requiring the use of fine dexterity with their hands are Very difficult while they remain in this form.

Any items being worn or carried by the Werewolf at the time of their transformation will be dropped. Some clothing may be destroyed by the process.

The Werewolf, whether they remain in control of their minds or not, will return to Human form when the sun next rises. They do not magically recover any damage they received while in wolf shape, and instead will take 1 level of Sanity damage after they are human again. They may attempt to Shrug this Sanity damage with a Hard Mind + Focus action.

Werewolves can only be killed if they are critically injured while in their wolf form. If their Health is critically injured while as a human they will appear dead, but as long as their corpse is not cremated, decapitated, or autopsied (an uncommon practice in Medieval times), they will return to life at the next sunrise with 1 Health level restored.

A Werewolf who has reached an age where they are likely to die just from being old, can only do so while in wolf form.

A Werewolf that dies, or is killed, in wolf form will have their body revert back to its human shape the next time no one is looking at it after it is discovered. They will remain dead, this time.

Werewolves can be created in one of three ways:

As a Curse upon someone who has committed an especially brutal act of murder or savagery. More than just a simple killing, mind you, but something truly shocking. Enough so that if witnessed by the Moon Goddess or by a Fairy King or Queen, they would place such a monstrous curse upon a mortal.

As an infectious Disease, contracted by those who are bitten by a Werewolf in their wolf form, and then fail to Shrug the damage afterwards. If they are killed by the Werewolf they will remain dead, only the survivors of a Werewolf attack need worry about gaining the curse.

As a dark Inheritance, for those who had a parent that was a Werewolf at the time of their conception. Their version of the curse does not become active until they reach adulthood. These Werewolves make their Mind + Focus action to remain in control after taking wolf form at Average difficulty.

Werewolves are Outlawed by both the Church and those who still follow the Old Ways, and are banned in both Human and Fairy settlements for the danger they pose if they lose control of themselves upon shapeshifting. Werewolves have to be extremely careful about getting indoors and staying indoors before the moon becomes visible, which does sometimes occur during the daylight hours. They must avoid windows as well, and when the moon is bright enough, being touched by a beam of its light at night when the sun doesn't diffuse it, is enough to trigger the transformation. No amount of willpower can halt or reverse the transformation once it has begun. If a Werewolf is seen in a Human or Fairy settlement there will typically be an investigation to determine who it was, and they will probably be arrested, tried, and executed by fire or decapitation.

Like other shapeshifters, the Werewolf Curse does bring with it the "benefit" of being immune to Metamorphosis magic, even if the spell or potion is intended to be beneficial.

WEREWOLF

Name: Level:
Role: Primary Skills:
Background: Primary Skills:

ATTRIBUTES/STATUS

BODY HEALTH

MIND SANITY

SPIRIT MORALE

SKILLS

BODY
Agility
Beauty
Strength

MIND
Knowledge
Perception
Technology

SPIRIT
Charisma
Empathy
Focus

COMBAT
Boxing
Melee
Ranged

STRANGE
Art
Languages
Science

MARTIAL
Dodge
Parry
Strike

PSIONICS
Clairvoyance
Psychokinesis
Telepathy

DIVINE
Blessing
Exorcism
Healing

OCCULT
Demonology
Metamorphosis
Necromancy

LIMITS

ENCUMBRANCE: DAILY PRAYERS:
MOVE/COMBAT: SPELL MEMORY:
MOVE/TRAVEL:

ITEMS

Armor: Weapon:
Other:
Spells:
XP:

SELKIE

God-fearing folk of the Sea, blessed with the gift to transform into Seals and Sea Lions.

CLASS: Church

Selkie Characters may be from either of the Human Church Roles of Clergy or Maiden. This will determine their Primary skills, as well as their Occupation and Equipment options.

Selkies can transform themselves into the form of a Seal or Sea Lion upon entering a natural body of water instantaneously as they submerge, if they choose to do so, and are not being observed by anyone within line of sight of them.

They recover all lost Status levels upon taking the form of a Seal or Sea Lion.

Upon taking their aquatic form, the Selkie must succeed on a Hard Spirit + Focus action, or they will lose control of themselves as they forget that they are really human, and go off to live life as an above-average pinniped for a number of Months equal to their Spirit Score. Once this time has expired, something will remind the Selkie of who they really are, and the Player may resume control of their Selkie Character to return them to land.

In seal form the Selkie can hold its breath for up to an hour at a time, dive to incredible depths, and can swim with amazing speed and agility. Selkies have Full Suit armor defense (Very difficult) while in the water thanks to their incredible reflexes and maneuverability. While on the shore in seal or sea lion form, their blubbery hide gives them Padded armor protection.

Selkies in their animal form gain a Bite attack that does an amount of Health damage equal to their Body Score. They cannot grapple, punch, kick, or use weapons as a pinniped. Their Bite attack is their only offensive ability.

Selkie who retain control of themselves in seal or sea lion form can choose to return to their human form anytime they come up for air at the water's surface, or otherwise leave the water by coming ashore. They do not recover any Status levels they lost while in seal form, and instead take 1 level of Morale damage. This Morale damage can be Shrugged off.

While in Seal or Sea Lion form, the Selkie uses the following Limit values:

ENCUMBRANCE: 1
MOVE/COMBAT: 2
MOVE/TRAVEL: 0
MOVE/SWIMMING: 2 + Body + Agility + Strength

Selkies can be killed in either Human or pinniped form, and their corpse will remain in that form. Most Selkies who die at sea are eaten by sharks or orca anyway, so the condition of their body doesn't matter than much under those circumstances.

Selkies are created in one of three ways:

They were blessed with the gift of shapeshifting by the Sea Gods, or a Mermaid Queen, who witnessed them attempting to save someone who was drowning or being attacked by a sea creature, in a situation that put themselves in great danger.

They are the offspring of a Selkie. Not all Selkies have Selkie children, only about 1 in 5 will share their parent's gift. Those that do will be able to shapeshift after reaching puberty.

They killed a Selkie in their pinniped form, and turned their hide into a coat or other garment that they then wore. The Sea Gods will curse them to have to take on their victim's life mission. The garment will only do this to its own murderer.

Known Selkies are accepted by both the Human Church and the Fairy Folk who dwell near coastlines, but they secretly worship the Sea Gods as the Mermaids do, and not God Almighty. In spite of this, they go completely unnoticed by the Church as pagan heretics, and are considered to be blessed individuals.

Selkies, like Werewolves and other Shapeshifters, can recover Status through natural healing processes at the same rate as normal Humans, as well as psychic surgery and Divine Healing magic. They are immune to Metamorphosis magic, including regeneration spells and potions.

SELKIE

Name:
Role:
Occupation:

Level:
Primary Skills:
XP:

ATTRIBUTES/STATUS

BODY   HEALTH

MIND   SANITY

SPIRIT   MORALE

SKILLS

BODY   **MIND**   **SPIRIT**
- Agility / Knowledge / Charisma
- Beauty / Perception / Empathy
- Strength / Technology / Focus

COMBAT   **STRANGE**   **MARTIAL**
- Boxing / Art / Dodge
- Melee / Languages / Parry
- Ranged / Science / Strike

PSIONICS   **DIVINE**
- Clairvoyance / Blessing
- Psychokinesis / Exorcism
- Telepathy / Healing

LIMITS

ENCUMBRANCE: DAILY PRAYERS:
MOVE/COMBAT:
MOVE/TRAVEL:

ITEMS

Armor: Weapon:
Other:

NYMPH

The Avatars of ancient and wise Trees, created to go out into the worlds of Man and Fairy, and try to live as one of them.

CLASS: Nobility
PRIMARY SKILLS: Strange

Nymph Characters are created using the same guidelines as a Human in the Nobility, with the Role of Lady. They will have the same Primary skills, and choices of Title, Archetype, and Equipment as Human Noble Ladies.

Nymphs are the psychic essence of a sentient Tree that is several centuries old, given a human form. They appear as adult women, and will exist for a number of years equal to their Spirit + Focus before they will disappear and return to their Tree in psychic form, to share their memories.

The Nymph avatar will remain as a psychic entity within the Tree in a state of slumber, sharing her memories, for a number of Decades equal to the number of years they were away from the Tree when they last returned.

Once this time has elapsed, the Nymph will awaken and regain her physical body as it had been when she returned to the tree, with any clothing or items she was carrying or wearing at the time she had vanished. She will appear near the base of the Tree, and will have to find her own way back to civilization and start a new life.

If a Nymph is Incapacitated in any of her Statuses, she will vanish and return to her Tree prematurely, and slumber an appropriate number of decades before she can return. The only way for a Nymph to die, is for her Tree to die. Not just the trunk, branches, and leaves. The roots themselves must be dead. Lighting strikes, fire, beavers, and Lumberjacks are all potentially deadly, and the Nymph will sense if her Tree is being mortally threatened. Most Nymphs try to remain close by.

In all other regards, a Nymph away from her Tree is identical to a human female, and they must eat and sleep and recover as a mortal would. They can become pregnant if they take a human lover. Their offspring are always human, but are highly likely to grow up to become a Wizard or Witch.

Many Nymphs elect to live in the forests where their Trees are located, where they can socialize with others of their kind, as well as with Satyrs and Fairy Folk whom they are friendly with. It is the Fairy Folk who believe them to have Noble status. Humans believe them to be Commoners, except for Magicians, and Satyrs and Mermaids consider them to be equals. Fairies consider them to be of the highest of ranks, just under the Swan Maidens in Nobility.

They are easily the most sociable of all the Inhumans, including those who live in Human settlements. They take a while in their first lifetime as a Nymph to get used to various human customs *and never quite develop a proper sense of modesty. But it is human life and lifestyles that the Trees that created them most want Nymphs to experience, even if they may be treated better by Satyrs and the Fairy Folk who live in and around the forests of their birth.*

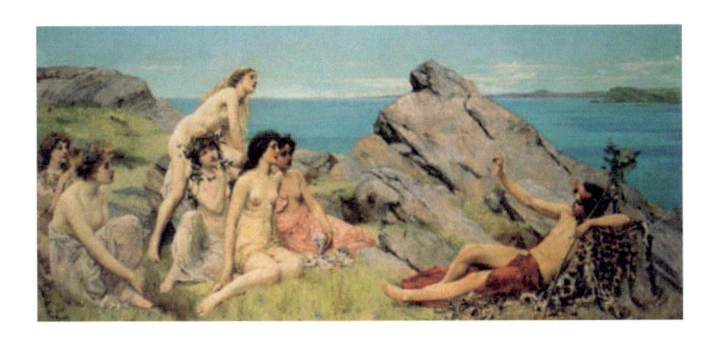

Nymphs possibly have the easiest time concealing their Inhuman natures than any other Fairy, Creature, or Beast. Their inevitable disappearance will often result in great tragedy and loss for those who knew them well, especially husbands and children. It sometimes takes a few lifetimes before Nymphs become conscious of this, and take steps to prepare their loved ones as their time runs out.

The Nymphs' mission gives them a lust for life that will spur them towards adventure, when the opportunity arises. They are also prone to trying new things and seeking out new experiences. They are not as depraved and bacchanalian as the Satyrs, but they are friends for a reason.

NYMPH

Name: *Level:*
Role: Lady   *Primary:* Strange
Title: *XP:*
Archetype: *Gold:*

ATTRIBUTES/STATUS

BODY   HEALTH
MIND   SANITY
SPIRIT   MORALE

SKILLS

BODY	*MIND*	*SPIRIT*
Agility	Knowledge	Charisma
Beauty	Perception	Empathy
Strength	Technology	Focus

COMBAT	*STRANGE*	*MARTIAL*
Boxing	Art	Dodge
Melee	Languages	Parry
Ranged	Science	Strike

PSIONICS	*DIVINE*	*OCCULT*
Clairvoyance	Blessing	Demonology
Psychokinesis	Exorcism	Metamorphosis
Telepathy	Healing	Necromancy

LIMITS

ENCUMBRANCE: DAILY PRAYERS:
MOVE/COMBAT: SPELL MEMORY:
MOVE/TRAVEL:

ITEMS

Armor: Weapon:
Other:
Spells:

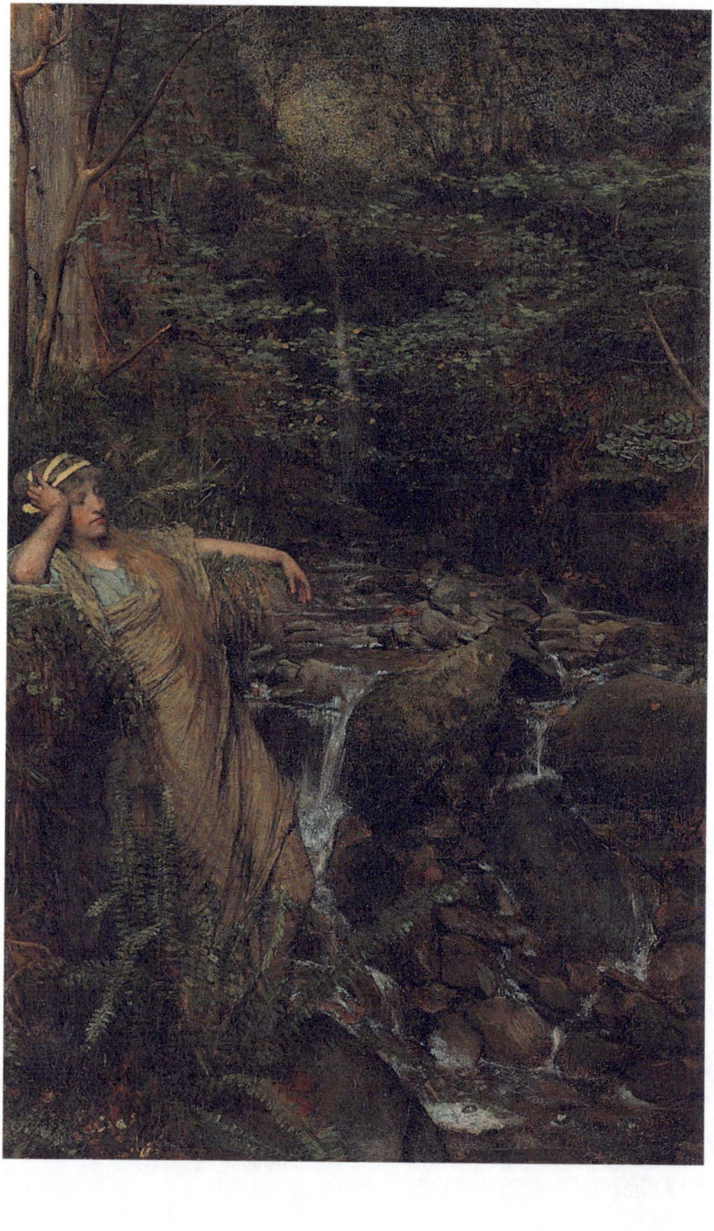

POOKA

Plain, Common Folk Cursed as Fools by Fairy Royalty, Pooka must learn to live with an Animal's Head.

CLASS: Commoner

Pooka Characters are created using the same guidelines as Human Commoners, with the same options of Role, Occupation, and Equipment.

Pooka are Humans that have been Cursed with powerful magic to live the rest of their lives with an animal's head in place of their own. They retain their intellect and skills, can still read and understand spoken words, but they cannot speak. Only animal noises appropriate to the species their head resembles will emerge when they try to talk.

Pooka must rely on writing and sign language in order to communicate with anyone, assuming they can understand even that. If they encounter someone with points in the Telepathy skill, and they attempt to open a mental link with the Pooka to speak Telepathically, the Pooka will be able to express themselves fully to the Telepath while the link is active.

Their head will be sized appropriately for a human body, but will otherwise look like the normal head of any natural animal. Donkeys, Foxes, Rabbits, Ravens, Toads, Snakes, Fish, Insects, and others are all possible. They will often reflect something about the Pooka's personality or ethics.

Pooka gain a +1D6 bonus to dice pools when using their Perception for actions regarding one specific sense, that the species whose head they possess is known to specialize: sight, hearing, smell, or taste.

Pooka have a Bite, Beak, or Horn attack that does an amount of Health damage equal to their Body Score.

Snakes and some Lizard and Fish Pooka may have a Venomous Bite, increasing their Bite damage by +2. They may only use their Venom bonus once every 24 hours.

Pooka attempting animal handling actions with animals of the same species do so at Easy difficulty.

Fish-Headed Pooka can breathe water or air.

Other aquatic Pooka can hold their breath for a number of hours equal to their Body Score.

In all other regards, Pooka are identical to Humans. If somehow a Pooka manages to find a mate and have children there is a 50/50 chance their offspring may be born as a Pooka. This applies even if two Pooka have children together.

Pooka are created in one of two ways:

They were a normal Commoner who was tricked into joining a Fairy Folk festival as their guest of honor; their King (or Queen) for a Day! Only to awaken after the party was over to find themselves Cursed as a Fool for a Lifetime, with their new head and Pooka features.

They are the child of a Fool for a Lifetime who inherited the curse. They may or may not have a head of the same species as their Pooka parent(s). These type of Pooka will always have regular human children, even if they mate with another Pooka. Pooka born to the curse tend to be less bothered by it. Those who are turned into Pooka can live miserable lives.

Pooka are immune to the effects of Metamorphosis magic. Their condition cannot be undone.

Pooka who were Fairy Fools will take 1 level of damage to their Sanity whenever they see their reflection clearly. They can Shrug this damage.

Pooka are officially Outlawed by the Church, as sinners who brought their curse down upon their own heads by straying form God's path, but they are accepted by the Common Folk, treated with pity slightly more often than disgust. Most ignore the Churchmen's ravings about the dangers of allowing Pooka to live among them. Only the cruelest of Nobles would have their men harass and persecute Pooka dwelling in their lands. But the Pooka life is a hard life nonetheless, especially for those who remember being human.

Unfortunately, while they would find the Fairy Folk more accepting of their strange condition, next to no Pooka would ever choose to live in a Fairy City. Many Pooka outwardly despise the Fairies for what they have done to them, and their association with other Shapeshifters hiding in Human society has had an effect on Fairy-Shapeshifter relations in general.

POOKA

Name: Level:
Role: Primary Skills:
Occupation: XP:

ATTRIBUTES/STATUS

BODY   ## HEALTH
MIND   ## SANITY
SPIRIT   ## MORALE

SKILLS

BODY
Agility
Beauty
Strength

MIND
Knowledge
Perception
Technology

SPIRIT
Charisma
Empathy
Focus

COMBAT
Boxing
Melee
Ranged

STRANGE
Art
Languages
Science

MARTIAL
Dodge
Parry
Strike

PSIONICS
Clairvoyance
Psychokinesis
Telepathy

DIVINE
Blessing
Exorcism
Healing

OCCULT
Demonology
Metamorphosis
Necromancy

LIMITS
ENCUMBRANCE: DAILY PRAYERS:
MOVE/COMBAT: SPELL MEMORY:
MOVE/TRAVEL:

ITEMS
Armor: Weapon:
Other:
Spell/Blessing:

CAT-SITH

The former Familiars of Wizards and Witches who have learned the secrets of magic and witchcraft.

CLASS: Nobility

Cat-Sith Characters are made using the same guidelines as Human Wizards or Witches. Their Social Class will be Nobility, even if the Character takes on the Role of Witch. All other aspects of their chosen Role's Primary skills, and their choice of Occupation and Equipment is identical to Human Magicians.

Cat-Sith are a breed of domestic cat that are descended from Magician's Familiars, that learned how to use magic and transform themselves into a Human body. Their descendants no longer require the use of spells to change their shapes.

Cat-Sith are born as Cats to Cat parents. Only one of their parents needs to be a Cat-Sith in order for their kittens to be Cat-Sith. Cat-Sith mothers must remain in cat form after becoming pregnant, and until their kittens are weaned. They tend to have small litters of only 3 of 4 kittens at most.

Once they have reached adulthood as a Cat, they will be ready to figure out how to shapeshift into their new human form, which will look like a young adult of the same gender as their Cat form. They will have to learn how to talk and walk, which will take several weeks or months, but soon enough they will be able to go around like a normal human and not raise too many eyebrows with odd behavior.

Cat-Sith age at the pace of the form they are in, and thus have incentive to spend as much time as possible in the longer-lived human form.

Cat-Sith can turn back into a Cat by concentrating for a Turn, while they are unobserved by anyone within line of sight of them.

Upon returning to Cat form, the Character must succeed on a Hard Mind + Focus action, or they will forget their human life, and wander off to be a normal Cat for a number of days equal to their Body Score, outside of their Player's control during this period. When the duration expires, the Cat-Sith will remember who they are and the Player may resume control of them.

Cat-Sith may change their shape back to their human form in the same manner as changing into a Cat: 1 Turn of concentration while unobserved.

Cat-Sith can recover at the normal rates of Status recovery in either of their forms, but whenever they shapeshift, to either Cat or Human, all of their lost Status levels will be restored. This can be extremely helpful when adventuring, but will not save them from old age catching up with them.

Cat-Sith can be effected by Metamorphosis spells, but can break out of them easily by shapeshifting into either their Human or Cat form, regardless of the spell's initial duration of effect.

While in Cat form, the Cat-Sith will use the following Limit values:

ENCUMBRANCE: Body -1
MOVE/COMBAT: 3 + Body + Agility
MOVE/TRAVEL: Body + Strength
MOVE/LEAP: = Body - (# of Items carried)

In Cat form, they receive a +1D6 Bonus to dice pools when using their Perception skill. They have excellent hearing and nightvision. Their natural reflexes and small size give them the equivalent of Full Suit armor defense (Very difficult to hit).

Their Cat form has both Claws and Teeth, but they are only lethal to creatures Cat-sized and smaller. Against Human sized opponents, their Bite or Claws can be used instead to make an attack on either their target's Sanity or Morale, (Player's choice), inflicting 1 level of damage to the selected Status, but made as a Boxing (Bite), or Melee (Claws) attack against their target's armor defense.

Cat's claws give Cat-Sith a +3 Bonus to Climbing.

In all other regards Cat-Sith are normal Cats, and would appear to be normal Humans when in that form, though they are apparently sterile with human partnering.

Cat-Sith are treated as Witches and Outlawed by the Church, who will often get the Nobility to support their demands to persecute them for witchery. Despite this a great many Cat-Sith live among humankind. However, almost half of their kind live amongst Fairy Folk, who consider the Cat-Sith to be Witch Nobility, and honorary Fairies. Perhaps one in every ten-thousand Cats in the world are Cat-Sith, but to those who know of them, they seem to be everywhere.

In spite of the fascination some humans have towards felines, the Cat-Sith can be very aloof and cruel. They are predators at heart, of one of the most successful predator species that ever walked the Earth. Given Human form and magical skills, they can be quite terrifying to those who cross their path. Several of the greatest and most evil of Witch Queens in history were secretly Cat-Sith.

Cat-Sith attempting animal handling with any feline species does so at Easy difficulty. Cat-Sith trying to control felines with Telepathy also do so at Easy difficulty

Cat-Sith are obsessed with magic and magical items. They will collect them if they find them, even if they cannot use them. They are also fond of books, and like Human magicians all Cat-Sith Characters are fully literate. They favor making their sanctums and ritual spaces in bookstores and libraries, instead of musty old Wizard's Towers or Witch's Huts.

The most serious flaws of the cat-Sith are their tendencies towards kleptomania and substance abuse. They love to steal trinkets and artifacts they see that they can pocket, and they love alcohol and narcotics. Even as Cats they will waste incredible amounts of time playing around rubbing catnip on themselves (Very difficult Mind + Focus to resist fresh catnip).

CAT-SITH

Name: Level:
Role: Primary Skills:
Occupation: XP:

ATTRIBUTES/STATUS

BODY   HEALTH

MIND   SANITY

SPIRIT   MORALE

SKILLS

BODY	MIND	SPIRIT
Agility	Knowledge	Charisma
Beauty	Perception	Empathy
Strength	Technology	Focus
COMBAT	**STRANGE**	**MARTIAL**
Boxing	Art	Dodge
Melee	Languages	Parry
Ranged	Science	Strike
PSIONICS	**DIVINE**	**OCCULT**
Clairvoyance	Blessing	Demonology
Psychokinesis	Exorcism	Metamorphosis
Telepathy	Healing	Necromancy

LIMITS

ENCUMBRANCE: DAILY PRAYERS:
MOVE/COMBAT: SPELL MEMORY:
MOVE/TRAVEL:

ITEMS

Armor: Weapon:
Other:
Spells:

209

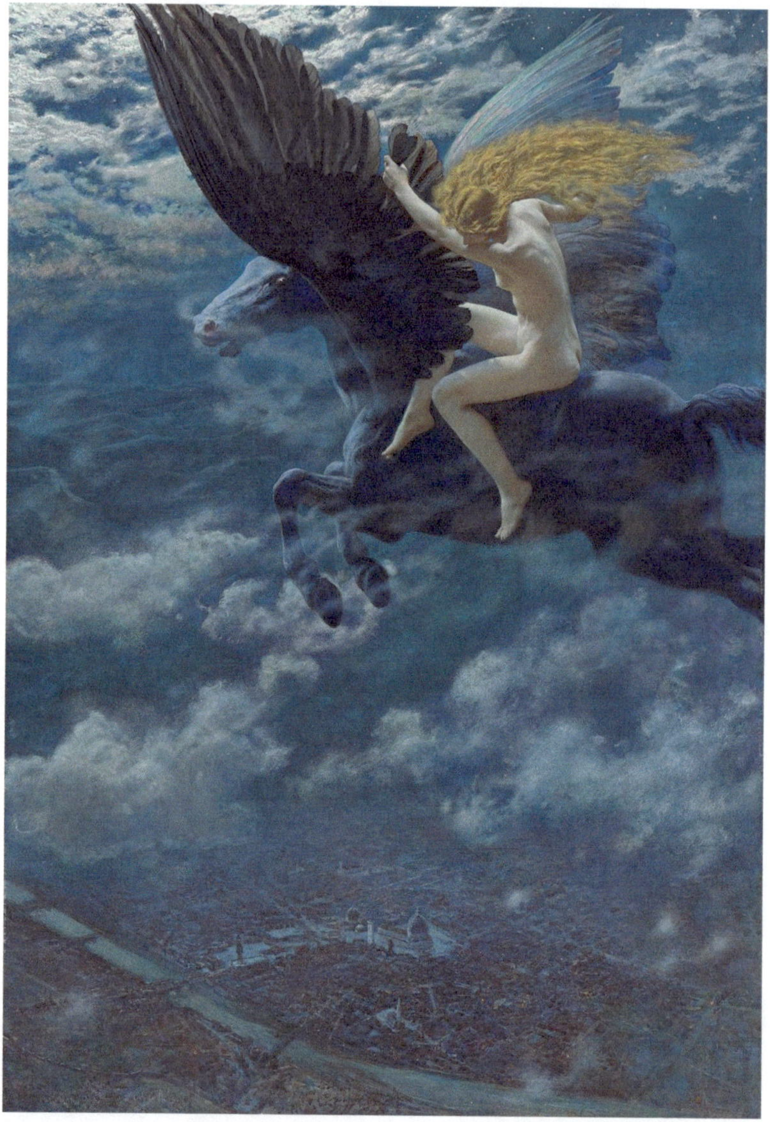

Fairy Foes

And so ends the portion of this Handbook that details options for Player Characters. The remainder of this book is for the Game Master.

Fairy Tale antagonists can and will include any of the Character types discussed previously in this book. Monsters are a mixed bag assortment of creatures, entities, and other Inhumans, who are generally hostile or dangerous to everyone they come in contact with. Those that are detailed in this Fairy Tale Handbook are as follows:

MONSTER	PAGE
Dragon	214
Wyvern	221
Sea Serpent	224
Giant	227
Troll	230
Ghost	234
Undead	237
Demon	248
Manticore	253
Griffon	257
Magic Horse	261
Intelligent Animal	270

Monsters and intelligent Foes in Fairy Tales are seldom disposable cannon-fodder, as depicted in fantasy after World War One. In Classic Fairy Tales, even a single wolf with no supernatural power can stand among the greatest of villains.

Fairy Tale Characters earn experience by encountering potential foes, and either defeating them with force of arms, or by forcing them to surrender, or by negotiating with them until they come around to take the Characters' side. Convincing any NPC to take a course of action that is against their natural interests and inclinations may also be worthy of an XP reward. XP rewards are based on the NPC's total number of combined skill points, they do not have levels of experience like Player Characters. XP rewards can either be split evenly between Characters who helped in the NPC or Monster's defeat, or each may receive the full XP Reward. The Choice is up to the Game Master and will effect how fast Players may level up their Characters. Shorter campaigns may want faster level progression.

Various animals and creatures have a range of Attributes that can seem superhuman, especially in the Body Score. They may also have a larger or smaller number of Health levels than they would normally have with their Body Score if they were a Player Character. Those that are non-sentient have access to a limited selection of skills compared to intelligent lifeforms.

Ghosts and Demons are spiritual entities, who have no Body Score or Health Status, and exist purely in the invisible Astral Space that covers the real world as beings of pure Mind and Spirit. They can cause trouble in Haunted locations, or possess the minds of the living. They are also used by Necromancers to create the Undead. Mortals almost always require magic or Exorcism to drive them away.

Fairy Tale Giants exist on a scale so large that they do not use Attributes or Status to determine the success of their actions, and they cannot be attacked by conventional means.

DRAGON

Ancient, sinister reptiles with flaming breath, Dragons guard their treasures in caves hidden near ponds, waterfalls, and wells.

Fairy Tale Dragons are an ancient and long-lived species of intelligent warm-blooded reptile, that dwells in underground caverns adjacent to small bodies of water. They can live for many centuries, sometimes even over a thousand years, and only once in all their lifetime will their females lay a clutch of eggs to hatch new Dragons into the world.

Dragons are a magical species, from sources far older than even the Fairy could remember. They can funnel a Pyrokinetic blast of fire via their breath, and can read and speak human languages, learn to use human and fairy objects and devices, and can even learn magical skills. The only thing Fairy Tale Dragons are lacking are the wings that 20th Century writers would start inventing for them, confusing Dragons and Wyverns in myth. Fairy Tale Dragons do not fly.

They will occassionally demand a virgin sacrifice to stop them from burning down a nearby town or village. What they do with the virgin varies from Dragon to Dragon. As an intelligent species, each Dragon has its own personality, agenda, and moral compass.

Dragons are Outlawed in most Human Kingdoms, though there have been instances of a Dragon being the power behind the throne a few times across history. Most of the time Humans will send a series of heroic fools to go slay Dragons when they are detected in their lands, until one of them manages to succeed. In Fairy Kingdoms Dragons are also seen as a menace to society, but are allowed to live in peace if the Dragon does not prove to be a constant problem.

Fairy Tale Dragons are not as massive in size as modern depictions would make you think. The largest and most ancient of their kind are only 30 feet long, from nose to tip of tail. The average adult dragon is somewhere between the size of a large dog, up to the size of a large horse or bull. Their legs are short, but carry them with surprising speed. Their long tails are whiplike and dangerous, and their heads sit on long necks, armed with bony horns on their brows, and fanged maws. They are fearsomely strong, with sharp claws and densely packed scales.

Their human-like level of intelligence, ability to use magic, and use verbal deceit and trickery make them formidable opponents.

An Adult Dragon will have 8 points for Attributes, with Scores as high as 6. Their Attributes begin with Scores of 1 prior to adding these points as with Player Characters.

A Dragon's Sanity and Morale are determined as normal (Attribute +2), but their Health Status is equal to their Body Score x2.

Dragons will have 20, 30, or 40 points in skills depending on their age, and may place these points in any skill, standard or magical, with the major exception of Divine skills, which no Dragon may learn. No skill may be raised higher than +5.

Dragons who have points in Occult skills will know a number of spells they can cast at Hard difficulty equal to their Mind + Knowledge. They do not need to all be determined at once when designing a Dragon NPC.

ENCUMBRANCE: 3 + Body + Strength
MOVE/COMBAT: Body + Agility
MOVE/TRAVEL: 10 + Body + Strength
MOVE/DIGGING: 1

The Dragon's scales makes them Impossible difficulty to hit. They are immune to fire damage, and only take half damage from cold effects.

On their Turn, Dragons may take one of the following actions: a Move Action, a Charge Attack followed by a Claw Attack, a Fire Breath Attack, A Claw Attack, or a Bite attack. They may also make a bonus Tail Lash Attack on the same Turn.

Dragons can breathe a Blast of Fire with a range equal to their Body Score, that does 2 Health damage per Turn, and may ignite flammable materials after 2 Turns of exposure. The range of their Fire Breath is equal to their Spirit Score.

Dragons with points in Psychokinesis can do an amount of damage with their fire breath equal to their skill bonus if it is +3 or higher.

Dragon claws used in a Melee attack do 2 points of Health damage. They will do an amount equal to their Strength skill if it is +3 or higher.

A Dragon's Bite Attack inflicts a number of levels of Health damage equal to their Body Score.

A Dragon's Tail Lash does an amount of damage to Health equal to the Dragon's Strength skill, and on a successful hit will also knock their target off their feet, who will be prone until their next Turn. Depending on the Dragon's size, the range for their tail can be between 1 and 3.

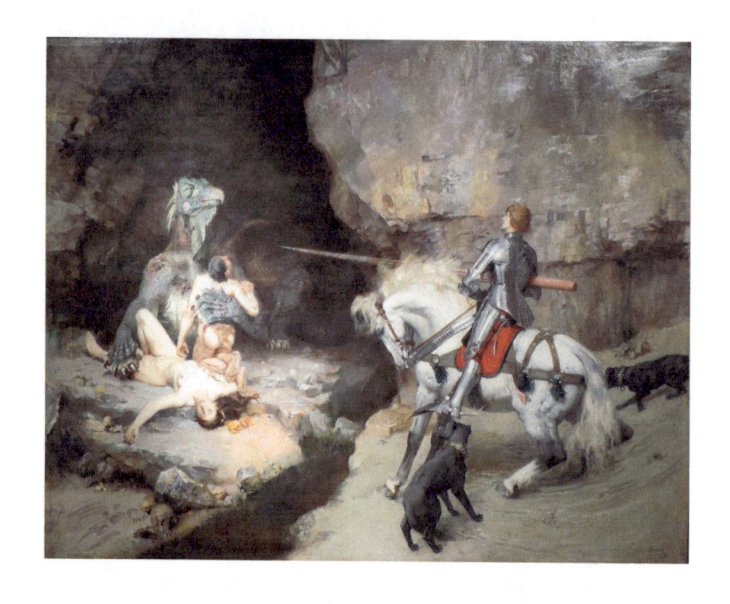

Dragons are deadly, cunning, and have no real exploitable weaknesses. More often than not it takes a Knight or Prince using their wits or appealing to the Dragon's greed that will win the day. But anyone who goes into a Dragon's den does so by putting their life on the line. Dragons are ancient and strange creatures, more alien to the human point of view than even the Fairy Folk.

WYVERN

The Lesser Dragons, Wyverns are gifted with flight, but have only an animal's intellect. They threaten the countryside and open wilderness.

Distant and primitive cousins of true Dragons, Wyverns have roughly the same amount of intelligence as a wolf or lion. They have a similar appearance and body-plan as a true Dragon, but their heads are more doglike, and in place of their forelimbs they have large membranous wings, like that of a bat.

Wyverns do not breathe fire, but have the same Claw, Bite, and bonus Tail Lash attack as a their Dragon kin, with Damage determined the same.

Wyverns have 4 points to add to their Attribute Scores (starting with Scores of 1). They may not raise their Mind or Spirit Scores higher than 2, and their Body Score may not be higher than 5. Their Health Status is Body x2.

Wyverns are non-sentient animals, and only have 5, 10, or 15 points for skills, depending on the Wyvern's age, selected from the following available options. No skill may be raised higher than +5.

WYVERN SKILLS
Agility	Strength	Perception
Charisma	Focus	Boxing
Melee	Dodge	

Wyvern scales provide them with Full Suit armor defense (Very difficult to hit).

Targeting one of their wings and inflicting 3 or more damage will force the Wyvern to land. They are very awkward and slow when grounded. Their wings only have Plated defense difficulty.

ENCUMBRANCE: 2 + Body + Strength
MOVE/COMBAT: = Body
MOVE/TRAVEL: 1
MOVE/FLIGHT: Body + Strength

Wyverns can live for a handful of centuries, if not slain, and mate for life, producing clutches of eggs every fifty to sixty years. They nest in the tallest and largest of trees, atop mountain bluffs, and in cliffs tucked high up on the faces of cliffs. They will range for many miles around their nest regularly looking for food. When their nest has eggs or hatchlings in it, they will also hunt down anything nearby that looks like it could be a threat to their young, often including innocent Common Folk.

SEA SERPENT

Close cousins of Dragons, Sea Serpents lurk in caves beneath the sea, hunting shipping lanes to sink boats for their plunder.

Sea Serpents fall somewhere between Dragons and Wyverns on the scale of intellect. They are related to both, but live far more isolated from either Human or Fairy civilizations, in the deep blue sea. They are the bane of Mermaids and Selkies, and other seagoing lifeforms. They are not smart enough to learn magic, but they are far more than mere beasts like the Wyverns. They are even greedier than Dragons, and do not care how many must die so they can get their coils around a freshly sunken treasure.

Sea Serpents have 6 points to add to their Attributes (starting at 1), with a maximum of 5 for their Body Score, and a maximum of 3 for their Mind and Spirit Scores. Their Health Status is Body x2.

Sea Serpents will have 10, 20, or 30 points for skills depending on their age. They can place points in any skill in the schools of Body, Mind, Spirit, Combat, and Strange. No skill may be raised higher than +5.

Sea Serpents do not have legs, and will suffocate under their own weight if left exposed out of the water for a number of hours equal to its Body Score. They range in length from 30 to 60 feet.

Sea Serpents only possess a Dragon's Bite attack and Tail Lash bonus attack, with damage determined in the same way as a Dragon's attacks.

Sea Serpents can breathe air and water indefinitely, with nearly unlimited depth tolerance.

Sea Serpents will have one or more horns on their head, that when used in a Charge Attack- inflict a Hull-damaging 5 points of damage.

Sea Serpents have softer skin than Dragons, their scales only provide them with Plated armor defense.

ENCUMBRANCE: Body + Strength
MOVE/SWIMMING: 2 + Body + Agility

Mermaids, Selkies, and coastal Human Kingdoms have united on multiple occasions throughout the centuries to hunt down and dispatch Sea Serpents that have been menacing their shared waters.

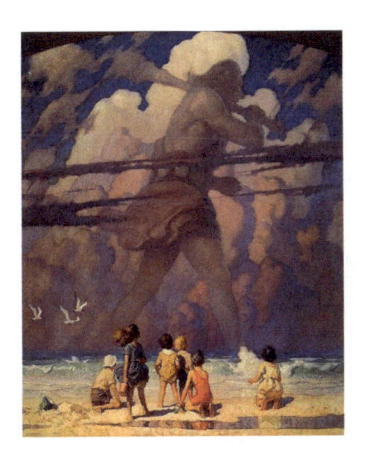

GIANT

Older than the Old Gods, a few surviving Giants still wander the Earth, or slumber for centuries at a time.

True Giants, and not "mere" Ogres and Trolls, exist on a scale that no longer relates to Attributes and Status and Skill rolls and Limits. They can stand hundreds of feet in height, as tall as the tallest buildings or Wizard's Towers ever constructed. As tall as what the modern reader would call a small to average size skyscraper.

Fairy Tale Giants may be flesh and blood creatures of a sort, but they are so huge that Human-scale attacks would maybe bother them as much as an ant-bite bothers us. Even magical spells that are not specially constructed large scale rituals requiring 6 or more spell casters to participate, will fail to effect a Giant automatically.

Even their sense of time-scale is incomprehensible to a Human or even Fairy. They are walking, sentient features of the landscape, not just a creature making a Move action. Their thoughts are alien and slow, unreadable to Telepaths. Speaking to them can take hours to days before they respond, if they respond at all.

Their speech is in the language of Giants, and fills the air with deep bass vibrations and cacophonies for up to days at a time. Carpenters must retroactively succeed on a Hard Mind + Technology roll to see if their buildings can withstand Giant speech within half a mile of its source.

Being struck by a Giant's attack is instantly lethal. They don't even do damage, they just destroy anything they touch unless they are deliberately being careful.

Defeating a Giant will always require creative thinking and use of non-traditional skills. They are worth 100xp if "defeated".

The pagan Old Ways religion followed by Witches and Fairies has its origins in the ancient worship of Giantkind, when they had enslaved mankind to make for them all the things their giant hands could not. Which was everything. They were deposed and slaughtered by the Old Gods, who were in turn deposed by God Almighty and His Son many thousands of years later.

TROLL

Rejects among Outcasts, Trolls are the mutant offspring of Goblins, forced to dwell in the wild, far from their kin.

Trolls are Lesser Giants, much like their Ogre cousins among the Fairy Folk. Trolls are the unofficial sixth form of Fairy, born from fratricide in utero to Goblin females too small to carry a full litter of Goblin pups to term. Trolls start off as oversized Goblins, and only grow larger and more unique as they get older. Most will be ejected from the Goblin Cities to find a home in the wilderness, living under bridges or huddling together in caves, when they find others of their kind. Trolls are sterile and cannot make new Trolls, which is good considering their strength and Fairy immortality, but they have a habit of gathering together in small groups which imitate mortal family roles.

Trolls can range anywhere between 8 and 20 feet tall. They grow in small increments every century or so of their existence. Those approaching 20 feet in height are truly ancient. The 8 foot tall ones are still effectively children by comparison, freshly booted from their Goblin hometown.

Trolls can have Body Scores as high as 5, and Mind and Spirit Scores as high as 2. They will have 4 points to add to their Scores (starting at 1).

Trolls will have 5, 15, or 25 skill points, depending on their age. They can place these points in any skill in the schools of Body, Mind, Spirit, Combat, and Psionics. No skill can be higher than +5.

Trolls use the following Limits:

ENCUMBRANCE: 3 + Body + Strength
MOVE/COMBAT: Body + Agility
MOVE/TRAVEL: 5 + Body + Strength

If any part of a Troll's body is touched by direct sunlight, they will transform into an immobile stone statue of themselves, until they are completely in shadow, or the sun has set. At which point they will return to their "natural" form and remember nothing that happened since the moment they froze.

Trolls can be smashed apart while in statue form, killing them instantly. They can only be harmed by bludgeoning weapons like hammers, or tools designed to break stone, and the difficulty of breaking them is equal to attacking something with Plated armor (Hard).

Trolls may not be invisible, but their strange collection of things they find to wear mixed with their own strange appearances make them Hard to detect with a Perception action when they are trying to hide. Impressive for something their size.

Trolls gain +1D6 to their dice pools for Perception actions involving their sense of smell.

A Troll's Punch or Kick inflicts 3 Health damage and knocks their target down. Their Bite requires a successful grapple first, and does a number of Health levels of damage equal to their Body -1.

Trolls survive mostly through banditry and theft. They will eat pets, livestock, and people, and are considered a major threat if reports get back to the King or Queen that Trolls plague their roads.

Unfortunately, getting rid of Trolls for good involves destroying any Fairy Circles in or near the Kingdom, an act that risks open war with the Fairy Kingdoms.

GHOST

Spirits of Nobles, Heroes, and Villains who continue on after death to Haunt those living in their domain.

Ghosts are detailed in the Total Party System Rules Handbook, and they follow the same rules in a Fairy Tale campaign, with Retreats and Gestalts, and a more fluid form of Occult magic than is practiced by mortals, as described in the section on Fairy Magic earlier in this book.

Ghosts feature frequently in Fairy Tales, as quest-givers, keepers of vital clues and secret information, as sympathetic pseudo-protagonists, and occasionally as the villain of the story. They have no body, exist outside of our dimension, and are capable of effecting the real world with psionics or by possessing the bodies of the living.

Ghost NPCs will have 3 points to add to their two Attributes: Mind and Spirit, which start with Scores of 1 just like mortals. Ghosts can have Attribute Scores as high as 4.

Ghost NPCs can conceivably know any skill, and will have 5, 15, or 25, skill points for average Ghosts of varying age. No skill can be raised higher than +5. They must have at least +1 in one Psionics skill.

Closely related to Ghosts are Phantoms, spirits which only have one Attribute, either Mind or Spirit, and its associated Status. Their Attribute can range between 1 and 3. They will have 5, 10, or 15 points in skills, most of which they will not be able to use.

Wisps are what happens to Ghosts and Phantoms who lose all of their Status levels, becoming sub-sentient orbs of floating light with no memories or identity. They have no Attributes, Status, or Skills.

Necromancers will use Binding spells to take Ghosts they have captured, or made a deal with, to create a variety of Undead.:

SPIRITS   UNDEAD
Wisp   Animated Skeleton
Wisp   Zombie Drone
Phantom   Zombie
Phantom   Vengeful Dead
Ghost   Familiar
Ghost   Ghoul
Ghost   Wight
Ghost   Mummy

Dealing with Ghosts requires the right magic skills, or a series of possibly hopeless fetch-quests.

UNDEAD

Mockeries of life, the Undead are made with corpses of mortals, reanimated with Ghosts and spirits.

The Undead rise due to the magic of Necromancy, or by being buried or left to slowly decay, at a location that is Haunted. All Undead require either a Ghost or Demon spirit to be bound to them to provide psychic force to move again, and provide thought and direction. The types of Undead are:

UNDEAD	SPIRIT	CORPSE
Animated Skeleton	Wisp	Skeleton
Zombie Drone	Wisp	Fresh or Rotting
Zombie	Phantom	Rotting
Vengeful Dead	Phantom	Fresh
Undead Familiar	Ghost	Animal
Ghoul	Ghost	Rotting
Wight	Ghost	Fresh
Mummy	Ghost	Prepared
Wraith	Demon	Skeleton
Demon Familiar	Demon	Animal
Dybbuk	Demon	Rotting
Thrall	Demon	Fresh
Vampire	Demon	Vampire

ANIMATED SKELETONS will only have Body Scores of 1, with 2 Health levels. They do not experience penalties from damage. They have no Mind or Spirit Score, or their associated Statuses. They will have 5 points for skills, which can be used on the following: Agility, Strength, Perception, Technology, Focus, Boxing, Melee, or Ranged. They can perform simple tasks given to them by their maker, and understand simple instructions. They only do damage by weapon used, their bony hands can scratch a target, but not enough to do significant damage, unless the Character is mobbed by a large group of skeletons at once.

ZOMBIE DRONES can be created using rotting of fresh cadavers, and use Wisps to make simple zombie automatons that will obey simple instructions from their creator. If left uninstructed they will go through the motions of their mortal life. Their Body Score will be between 1 and 3, and their Health is Body +2. They have no Mind/Sanity or Spirit/Morale. They have 5 points for skills, which can be chosen from the same ones Animated Skeletons may know.

A regular ZOMBIE is intelligent, but still completely obedient to their maker's commands. They are made from bodies that have started to noticeably decay, and cannot pass for a living human. They will only have Body and Mind Scores, which start and 1, and they have 3 points to divide between them. Their Health and Sanity Statuses are Attribute +2. Zombies will have 10 Skill points in any skill from the schools of Body, Mind, Spirit, Combat, Strange, or Psionics. No skill may be raised higher than +5.

VENGEFUL DEAD are made from Corpses that are still fresh enough to pass for living if not examined closely. The Phantoms that empower them are selected for their anger and wrath, and are sent to hunt down living targets who offended either the Phantom, or their master. They will have 3 points to split between their Body and Spirit Scores (which start at 1). Vengeful Dead will have Body Scores of 2 or 3, and 10 skill points to select from the following schools of skills: Body, Mind, Spirit, Combat, Strange, and Psionics. No skill may be raised higher than +5.

An UNDEAD FAMILIAR is a Wizard or Witch's (most often Witches) pet or animal companion. What separates a Familiar from an average pet is that the Familiar is an animal that had a Ghost bound to it immediately after its death, to give it human intelligence and a psychic bond with the occultist who created it. Undead Familiars will have 3 points to add to all 3 Attributes, which start with Scores of 1, and cannot be raised higher than 3. Their Status levels are the standard Attribute+2, and like all Undead they do not suffer penalties from damaged Status. They will have 15 skill points which may be added to any skill except in the Divine school. No skill may be raised higher than +5. The Limits for a typical small animal are as follows:

ENCUMBRANCE: 1
MOVE/COMBAT: 3 + Body + Agility
MOVE/TRAVEL: = Body
MOVE/FLIGHT*: 5 + Body + Agility

*Winged animal species only

A GHOUL is an Undead made from a Ghost bound to a noticeably rotting corpse. They have far more autonomy from their creators than Undead made from Wisps and Phantoms. They will have 3 points for Attributes, Mind, Body, and Spirit, which start with Scores of 1. Their Status is Attribute+2. They will have 15 points to add to skills in the schools of Body, Mind, Spirit, Combat, Strange, and Psionics. No skill may be raised higher than +5.

A Ghost bound to a fresh, recently deceased corpse that can pass as living unless examined closely is known as a WIGHT, and is made in the same manner as a Ghoul.

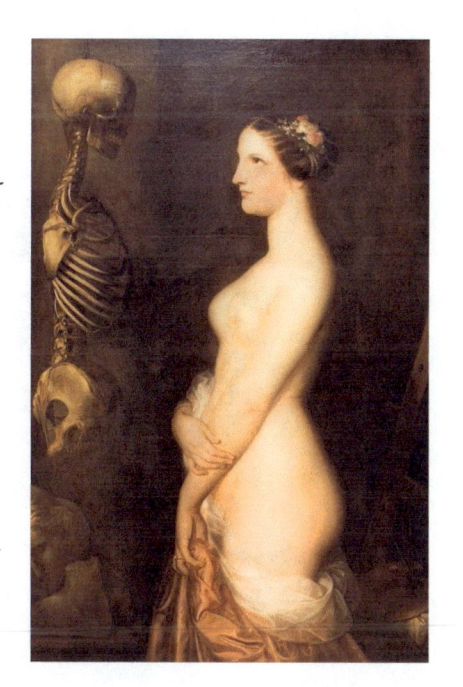

A MUMMY is made by Binding a Ghost into a body, (often its own), that has been ritually prepared and preserved with Science (Very difficult), prior to the ritual to bind the ghost being cast. Mummies appear like a living person for many centuries before decay starts to finally set in. They have 5 points for their Attributes, (starting at 1), which can be raised as high as 5. They will have 20, 35, or 50 skill points depending on how long they have existed since their creation. They may place these points into any skill. No skill may be raised higher than +5.

WRAITHS are Animated Skeletons created with a demon spirit instead of a Wisp. They are exponentially more intelligent and dangerous than a plain Animated Skeleton. They will have 5 points for their Attributes. Their Health Status is equal to their Body Score. Their Sanity and Morale are Attribute+2 as normal. Wraiths have 10 points for skills in the Psionics and Occult schools, and 5 additional points for skills in any category except Divine. They must use Telepathy or Psychokinesis to speak.

DEMON FAMILIARS are like normal Undead Familiars, created in the same way, just with a Demon instead of a Ghost. They will have 10 points for Psionics and Occult Skills, and 5 points for skills in any other category except Divine. No skill may be raised higher than +5. The biggest difference between Undead and Demon Familiars is that the Demon Familiars are constantly looking for a way out of their Binding spell, or to sabotage their master's works without breaking the restrictions of the Binding and Command spells placed upon them.

DYBBUK are Ghouls made with Demons instead of Ghosts. They have 5 points for Attributes, which can go as high as 5. They will have 10 points in Psionics and Occult skills, and 10 points in any skill in the other schools, except Divine. No skill may be raised higher than +5. Dybbuk are often set free by their creators to raise havoc among the living. They are unnecessarily cruel and vicious to those they victimize.

A THRALL is the Demonic equivalent of a Wight, and are typically created to be one of their Creator's servants or spies. They have the same Attribute and Skill points as a DYBBUK.. They can delay their body's decay by drinking human blood at least once a week. Failure to do so will make them start to resemble a corpse, and after another week without feeding they will become a Dybbuk instead.

All Undead made from Ghosts, and the Demonic Undead of Wraiths, Demon Familiars, Dybbuk, and Thralls, can only recover lost Health levels by trading their Sanity or Morale levels to replenish their Health. Ghost Undead will have to go to their Ghost's Retreat to recover their Sanity and Morale. Demons recover their Sanity and Morale at a rate similar to humans.

Only Thralls can extend the lifelike appearance of their body by drinking human blood regularly. It gives them no other benefits from drinking it.

VAMPIRES are created by binding a Demon to a corpse that has been prepared through ritual torture, moments after its death. The Vampire will have to feed on human blood once per month in order to sustain its body's ageless appearance. Failure to do so will cause the Vampire to start losing a point from their Body Score every month that they do not feed until it reaches 0 and they crumble to dust and die. Feeding on blood again will restore their lost Attribute points. They do not recover naturally, and need to drink blood from a live human to replenish their lost Status levels with the Health levels they drink from their victim. Vampires have fangs that give them a Bite attack that does 1 health damage, and allows them to drain 1 Health level from their target for each subsequent Turn that they can maintain a grapple, if the victim is unwilling.

Vampires have 6 points for their Attributes, and 30, 40, or 50 points to add to skills in any category except for Divine. They will always have some of those points placed in Psionics and Occult skills.

Vampires whose Health becomes Incapacitated enter a corpse-like state, and will awaken at sunset three days later with 1 Health level restored. They can only be killed by starvation, by fire damage, by decapitation and/or extreme dismemberment, or by exposure to the light of the sun, which inflicts 1 level of Health damage per minute of exposure (2 Turns).

Why Vampires were originally created is unknown. Their elders learned the spells to make more of their kind, and Vampires have largely been in charge of their own creation for centuries, if not thousands of years. Thankfully they are rare, and careful about creating too many of themselves.

DEMON

Malicious spirits that plague the living, Demons are jealous and hateful beings born from pure psychic potential, and unleashed to corrupt the innocent.

Demons take many forms and guises, for there is no singular kind of Demon. Most are just average spirits who have been classed all together by the teachings of the Church in Fairy Tale settings. In form and function and identity, the Demons are truly legion.

Spirits are like Ghosts in that they are disembodied sentient entities held together by psionic energies and determination to maintain their existence.

Spirits are not like Ghosts in that they were never once living beings of physical matter. They came into existence in a multitude of ways: the interplay of inter-dimensional physics, recurrent dreams, avatars of ancient gods, servants of light and dark, servants of the self. They arrange themselves in imitation of life, separating themselves into different pantheons and lineages and species.

Spirits believe all manner of things about themselves, and all of it is lies. Not necessarily intentional in their deceit, but their portrayal of who they are and where they come from has changed and morphed over the ages of History, shaped by the beliefs of the mortals the spirits both covet and despise.

Fairies are spirits. As are Cherubs and Nymphs. Even Vampires can be described as spirits-made-flesh, though in a cheater's fashion. They, and those like them, have purchased a more solid sense of themselves by taking on a physical form, and dwelling in the mortal's world. The rest live in an endless storm of melting consciousness, and in their own way, the Church is correct to damn them all as Demons and Corruptors.

Demons in their natural disembodied form can choose to appear psychically as nearly anything. Only when confronted outside of any mortal mind they may possess can a Demon be destroyed, and it is always through words and argument. Unlike Ghosts, who cannot be reduced any further than existence as a Wisp, Demons will be undone if both their Sanity and Morale are destroyed.

Characters in Fairy Tales rarely are given opportunities to destroy such a foe permanently. To confront a Demon in their natural state, they must be tracked down to their lair within Astral Space, or one of the other dimensions of Heaven or Hell. Demons in Fairly Tales, more often than not, are possessing entities who have taken control of someone or another to spread horror and misery to the real world.

They can be driven out and the day is saved, but eventually they always come back.

Demons can come in a variety of flavors and identities, but such details are more a matter of cosmetics or philosophy. Whatever a spirit calls itself, or associates with, they are all designed as NPCs in a manner nearly identical to Ghosts: They only have Mind and Spirit Attributes, and Status levels for Sanity and Morale (Attribute+2). These Attributes start with Scores of 1, and they will receive 6 points to add to them. Demons may only raise their Attributes as high as 6. They will have 10 points minimum placed in skills in the Psionics and Occult categories. They will have an additional 5, 10, or 15 points in skills in the schools of Body, Mind, Spirit, Combat, Strange, Psionics, and Occult, depending on how often they have been able to spend time possessing living people to acquire mortal skills. No skill may be raised higher than +5. They use magic in the same manner as Ghosts and Fairies, and many are skilled at possession techniques, but most of their quirks and restrictions are self-imposed by their own beliefs about what they are. If a ring of salt keeps a demon out of your house, the power is not in the salt, the ritual circle, or even the beliefs of whomever made it. It is the Demon's own belief that there are Rules that it must Obey, and one of them involves simple everyday salt. The Church acknowledges a handful of spirit-types, such as the Cherubs and Seraphim, as Angels rather than Demons, but is there really any difference between Seraphim and Balseraph? Like any antagonistic force in a Fairy Tale, a Demon should be a unique entity with its own personality and goals, even if those goals wouldn't make sense to a mortal human. The only common denominator with Demons and any spirit, is a deep sense of envy towards the living. Envy can excuse quite a few atrocities.

MANTICORE

Beasts made from men, or men made from beasts?

Manticores were once mortal men and women who had caused great offense or disruption at a festival or ritual ceremony held by the Fairy Folk, and had been Cursed by the Fairy King or the Fairy Queen to become beasts outside to match the beast within. Or so the story goes.

Whether it be by Fairy or Human hands, Manticores are the results of Metamorphosis magic being employed to shape the flesh of humans into that of a monster, who is driven mad with the indignity of what they have become until they wind up as mindless, murderous beasts living out in the hinterlands of civilization, stalking and preying upon the weak and helpless.

Average spells of Change Species or Monstrous Visage do not make someone into a Manticore. They are a combination of spells added together, including those to change their body to that of some predatory animal like a lion or a wolf, yet to keep their human face mostly intact while giving them a mouth full of sharpened fangs and sharklike teeth. Many will also have quilled spines growing along their spine and shoulders, and barbed hooks on their tails like a scorpion's sting.

They would be robbed of their ability to talk, but were left just intelligent enough to understand the things people would say of them. Enough to feel the horror and revulsion themselves when they caught a glimpse of their reflection in a puddle.

Manticore are thankfully rare, and they cannot breed to make more of themselves. They can only be created via magic. They remain mortal and will age and die as they would have prior to their transformation into their Manticore form.

A Reset Form spell cast upon them will return them to their original human body, but their mind will be forever ruined by their experiences. They will remain beastial and bloodthirsty for the rest of their lives, and may never relearn how to speak again. Some consider it more kind to kill them in their Manticore form, than to try to restore them.

Manticore will only have dim memories of the skills they once had. They will have 10 points in skills from the schools of Body, Mind, Spirit, Combat, or Strange. They are now a superhuman predator.

Manticore have Body Scores of 4, and their Mind and Spirit Scores are both 1. Their Status levels are determined as normal (Attribute+2), but their Sanity is permanently 0. They have Human Limits.

Manticore have thick fur and spines on their back, giving them Plated armor defense. They have humanlike fingers and toes on their paws, and do not have a claw attack. They can use rudimentary tools with their forepaws.

A Manticore who successfully Grapples a target can use their Bite attack in them for each Turn they can maintain the Grapple. Their Bite does 4 levels of Health damage.

A Manticore with a Tail Barb can use it to Sting a close range target for 1 level of Health damage. The target must then make a Hard Body + Strength action or take 3 Health damage on their following Turn from the sting's poison. Only 1 in 4 Manticore will be equipped with a stinger.

Manticores are somewhat suicidal. If faced with a heroic opponent who seems to have what it takes to finish the job, a Manticore may deliberately give them opportunities to land the fatal blow. If the hero seems weak however, the Manticore will be filled with rage and show them no mercy.

GRIFFON

Terror of the Sky and King of Beasts, Griffons are immortal guardians of once-sacred places. Old, gone feral, and dying.

Griffons are strange but seemingly natural creatures who were more common in ancient times, and were believed once to be sacred and immortal. To this day their image adorns many a banner, flag, and sigil to indicate royalty, strength, and power. Yet even by the age of Fairy Tales, Griffons had fallen on hard times. Their treasures and nests had been raided by Greek Heroes. Their mountain valleys were settled by shepherds and farmers. Their great trees in the forest were the first to be felled by lumberjacks and set to the mills. In spite of living incredibly long lives, they did start to die, and fewer and few eggs hatched every century.

But they are not all yet gone from this world. You may still find one here and there, hiding in the wild places of this world. Old, and in pain, and nasty about it. Fairy Folk encounter them more than Humans nowadays, and they know it is best not to spend too much time in range of their dens and hiding places. Those that they can, they will try to befriend, leaving sacrifices and food and little trinkets for them to hoard out where they can be found, to keep the peace between the Griffon and whichever Fairy settlement neighbors them.

Griffons are as close to being fully sentient as any beast can get. They understand language, and can even speak in limited fashion, with far more understanding of what they are saying than you'd find in birds like Ravens. They do not use tools, yet seem instinctively driven to hoard human-made items and trinkets and coins, and watch over them once they have been safely moved to their mountain stashes. Griffons are extremely resistant to efforts to tame, domesticate, or train them. Only the greatest heroes of history have ever managed to ride one. They're much like cranky people.

Griffons are winged creatures and can fly at speeds of up to 100 miles per hour. Much like a Swan Maiden, they need space to take off and land, and must focus on what they are doing when cruising below 50 feet in altitude. They cannot hover in place, and must stay in motion while airborne.

Griffons have catlike claws which inflict 2 levels of Health damage with a normal attack. An Aerial Charge Attack using their Claws will inflict 4 levels of damage and knock their opponent down/out of the air.

A Griffon's powerful beak gives them a Bite Attack that does 3 levels of Health damage to a grappled/pinned target.

The Griffon's strong feathers give them Plated armor defense when on the ground. When flying, they have Full Suit armor defense.

Griffons have extremely long-distance high resolution vision. They receive +2D6 to dice pools when making a Perception action using vision.

Griffons will have 6 points for their Attributes. Their Body Score can be as high as 5, and their Mind and Spirit Scores may be as high as 4. All Scores start at 1 before points are applied.

Griffons will have 25 points for skills in the schools of Body, Mind, Spirit, and Combat. They will also have an additional 5 points for skills in the Psionics and Divine categories.

ENCUMBRANCE: Body + Strength
MOVE/COMBAT: 2 + Body + Agility
MOVE/TRAVEL: 1 + Strength
MOVE/FLIGHT: 5 + Body + Strength

MAGIC HORSE

Of course, of course.

Horses are a stable of Fairy Tale fiction. While many animals have their intelligent variants who pop up in some stories, Horses have appeared time and again, endowed with abilities beyond speech and reason, and in four species: Winged Horses, Fairy Horses, Sea Horses, and Fire Horses.

WINGED HORSES, sometimes called Pegasuses, are smart but non-sentient horses who have large feathered wings that allow them to fly, but are otherwise normal animals of their species. Most are wild, migrating egg-layers, who don't handle captive breeding well, and have never been domesticated. They can be tamed and trained by proficient handlers, and are common enough to still be seen from time to time in the possession of some knight or nobleman of Human or Fairy origin.

FAIRY HORSES, commonly known as Unicorns, are famous but extremely rare angelic Horses with a single horn growing from their heads, reminiscent to that of a narwal. They are Fairy Horses, immortal, and made of the same psychic matter as other Fairy Folk. They are sentient, but never speak, and are considered to be one of the most sacred of beings by followers of the Old Ways. Unicorns live and die by the same rules as the Fairies. Those who seek to hunt them for their horn always turn up empty handed, even if they were successful in finding and killing the beast. Unicorns never allow themselves to be used as beasts of burden, even in an emergency, or for someone they care for.

A SEA HORSE, also known as a Kelpie, are aquatic Horses that can breathe both water and air, and are often domesticated by Mermaids to serve as mounts and beasts of burden. They have finned hooves, and seem to run through the water and waves as if on land. They are not sentient, possibly not even as intelligent as normal horses.

They graze on kelp and sea weed, and wild herds of their kind roam along the coastlines of many lands.

FIRE HORSES are enchanted creatures that have manes of living fire, and leave flames behind with every hoof step. They are favored as mounts by the Undead, and other beings who have little fear of fire's touch. Most Fire Horses live in wild herds in the far north, and are given a wide berth by local predator species.

TALKING HORSES would technically fall under the category of Intelligent Animals, which may be amazing, but are not magical unless they have learned magic skills. Since we're talking about other super-horses here though, we may as well mention that every once in a while a foal is born to normal horse parents, who will grow up to have human-like intelligence, and the ability to speak. They are otherwise perfectly average horses in every other regard.

Your basic, normal Horse has a Body Score as high as 4, a Mind Score as high as 2, and a Spirit Score as high as 3. They will have 4 points to add to their Attribute points, starting with Scores of 1. A normal Horse will have 10 points in skills, chosen from: Agility, Beauty, Strength, Perception, or Boxing. No skill may be higher than +5. A Horse can carry a number of average-weight human riders equal to its Body Score -1. For each passenger not being carried, a Horse may add +5 to its Encumbrance if the items are in a bag or tied down. Horses can also be harnessed to wheeled carts and pull them at half their normal speed (round up), or to a wagon with one or more other Horses (slowest horse's full Move Limit). A Horse can kick with its rear legs at targets located behind them for a number of Health levels in damage equal to their Strength bonus. A Horse's Bite does 1 level of Damage to either Health or Morale (Horse's choice). A Stomp or Trample (Charge Attack) with their hooves does an amount of Health damage equal to their Body Score. Horses have no natural armor defense.

A standard Horse's Limits are as follows:

ENCUMBRANCE: 5 + Body + Strength
MOVE/COMBAT: 3 + Body + Agility
MOVE/TRAVEL: Body + Strength

Horses need large amounts of food and water per day compared to humans, and can exhaust themselves to death much easier if they are not allowed to rest at least every other leg of their journey, as defined in miles by their Move/Travel Limit. Horses that are pushed to keep going for more than 3 rest periods will have to succeed on a Hard Body+Strength action with each subsequent time they skip a rest to keep moving. Failure means the Horse dies from being overtaxed.

A Horse's rider gives directions to the Horse with a Body + Charisma action, with a difficulty based on how much the Horse likes their rider:

FEELINGS TOWARDS RIDER	DIFFICULTY
Hates	Impossible
Dislikes	Very
Stranger	Hard
Likes	Average
Loves	Easy

The rider need only roll to control or direct the animal if a sudden change in direction or speed is called for, or for in tense situations like combat.

When not actively commanding the Horse, the Rider may use their Turn to take any action they could accomplish on horseback, including weapon attacks, or even the casting of spells. This freedom of being able to have the Rider attack while the Horse makes a Move action is in part why horse-mounted cavalry and warriors have always had an edge against opponents on their feet.

A Winged Horse uses the same guidelines as a normal Horse, with the following Limits:

ENCUMBRANCE: 5 + Strength
MOVE/COMBAT: 1 + Body + Agility
MOVE/TRAVEL: = Body
MOVE/FLIGHT: 3 + Body + Agility - (# of Riders)

Fairy Horses have a Horn that can be used to do 2 levels of Health damage with a Melee Attack. Their Attribute Scores may be as high as 5, and they will have 8 points to add to their starting Scores of 1. Fairy Horses will have 10 points in Psionics and Divine Skills, and an additional 20 points in skills from the schools of Body, Mind, Spirit, and Strange. No skill may be raised higher than +5. They cannot bear the weight of a Rider, or any significant cargo. Attacks with their dainty hooves only do 2 points of damage. Fairy Horses use the following Limit values:

ENCUMBRANCE: = Strength
MOVE/COMBAT: 3 + Body + Agility
MOVE/TRAVEL: 2 + Body + Strength

Sea Horses can breathe both air and water, and must breathe at least a bit of both every day. If on land, they will need to go to the water, and if at sea, they will need to come up to the surface, if only for just a few quick breaths. Sea Horses are comfortable in both salt and freshwater environments. They are covered in scales and have bony, hornlike protrusions on their brows. They have a natural Plated armor defense, and their bony horns can be used in a Charge Attack to do 3 levels of Health damage. They cannot use their hooves for a Stomp, Trample, or Kick attack while submerged underwater. When on land, these attacks do the same amount of damage as a terrestrial horse. They have the same attributes and skill options as a natural horse. A Sea Horse uses the following Limit values:

ENCUMBRANCE: Body + Strength
MOVE/COMBAT: Body + Agility
MOVE/TRAVEL: 1 + Strength
MOVE/SWIMMING: 3 + Body + Agility

Fire Horses are the most obviously magical of the Magic Horses. Their mane is made out of magical flames, which will do 2 levels of Health damage per Turn of contact, and can set flammable objects on fire after 2 Turns of contact. Their hooves drip fire with every step, which will burn out after 1 Turn unless they are on a flammable surface, such as wood or dry grass. Their singed hides have been toughened by heat to give them Padded armor defense. Attacks with their hooves do an additional 2 levels of fire damage to Health. They are immune to both fire and cold attacks. Their fiery mane and hoof effects cease if they are killed. They are, in every other regard, normal horses.

Talking Horses may raise their Mind and Spirit Scores as high as 3, and will have 5 points for attributes (starting at 1, Body as high as 4). They will have 10, 15, or 20 points for skills in the schools of Body, Mind, Spirit, Strange, or Divine. Horses with Divine skills are likely to also have taken a Vow of Silence. In all other regards they are normal Horses.

INTELLIGENT ANIMAL

Was not Goldilocks the Villain of the Tale?

Intelligent individuals among species of beast normally considered lesser than the sentient races are born in small numbers with every generation, mostly to animals who dwell in lands touched by Fairy magic in some form or another. These creatures can learn how to talk, and even use tools and items to a limited degree, but they remain beasts all the same. Many resent and even hate both Humans and Fairies for making prey of them and their kin. From the Wolf that is now hunting the hunters, to the Rabbit who dreams of uplifting his fellow rabbits to build a civilization to rival that of Man's, the motives of intelligent animals are as many and as varied as any other people.

Most non-sentient species of animals of mouse size and larger will have a maximum Limit on both their Mind and Spirit Scores of 2, while their Body Score maximum is largely determined by their size. The majority of animals will only have a Mind or Spirit Score of 1. Even the smart ones are only smart in a relative sense. They cannot reason or understand the way Humans and Inhumans can. They are also limited in what skills they may place points in. A few species of bird can memorize and halfway understand Human languages, and many domestic animals learn to recognize certain words and learn commands, but they are not capable of true Language, and without it, true Thought.

Intelligent mutants who are born to roughly 1 in 500,000 animals of any given species can learn how to understand real Language, and speak it as well. They can also learn a much larger amount of possible skills, and can attempt to use Human or Fairy tools and objects at Hard or Very difficult, if they have points in Technology. They can raise their Mind and Spirit Scores as high as 3.

The volume of possible animal species is both tremendous in scope, yet also terribly redundant. Insects, Reptiles, Fish, Arachnids, Amphibians, Birds, Mammals, all are possible. Some may have special talents like water breathing or winged flight, or natural weapons like teeth, beaks, claws, and talons. Some may be poisonous. For simplicity's sake, when designing an Animal or an Intelligent Animal NPC, use the creature's Size first to determine its Attribute range, and then plug in special abilities as appropriate for its species. Non-sentient animals will have 5 or 10 points in skills, selected from the following:

ANIMAL SKILLS
Agility
Beauty
Strength
Knowledge
Perception
Charisma
Empathy
Focus
Boxing (Grappling/Bite attacks)
Melee (Claw/Appendage attacks)
Clairvoyance

Non-Sentient animals have Sanity and Morale Status equal to their associated Attributes.

TINY ANIMALS

Ranging from creatures the size of Mice down to insects, Tiny Animals have Body Scores no higher than 1, (minimum 0), and No Health Status. Any attack that hits them is instantly lethal if from a human sized attacker. Boxing can be used for non-lethal attempts to catch a Tiny Animal. Their attacks do not do enough damage to count as a Health level, even if they draw blood. Tiny Animals can hurt Player Character sized creatures if they are venomous. They are Very difficult to hit due to their size and reflexes.

SMALL ANIMALS

Ranging in size from a Rat to a Fox or Medium sized dog, Small animals can have Body Scores as High as 3 (minimum 1). Their Health Status is equal to their Body Score, but they do not suffer penalties until they have taken damage, if their Status when undamaged is lower than Optimal. Small animals can sometimes inflict enough damage to lower a target's Health by 1 level. Some may use their attacks to lower a target's morale instead. They are Hard to hit due to their size.

MEDIUM ANIMALS

Ranging in size from a large dog up to a pony, this is the size Category where Humans are located. Medium animals can have Body Scores as high as 5, and their Health Status is Body+2.

LARGE ANIMALS

Ranging in size from a Pony up to a Hippopotamus, Large Animals may have Body Scores as high as 6. Their Health Status remains at Body +2.

GIANT ANIMALS

Giant Animals range in size from an Elephant up through whale-sized creatures. Their Body Scores can be as high as 8, and their Health Status is Body x2. Giant Animals will often find Agility actions to be Very difficult or Impossible.

SIZE	ATTRIBUTE POINTS
Tiny	1
Small	2
Medium	5
Large	6
Giant	8

TINY LIMITS
ENCUMBRANCE: 0
MOVE/COMBAT: 1
MOVE/TRAVEL: 1
*MOVE/LEAP: 1
*MOVE/FLIGHT: Body + Agility
*MOVE/SWIMMING: 3 + Body + Agility

SMALL LIMITS
ENCUMBRANCE: 1
MOVE/COMBAT: 3 + Body + Agility
MOVE/TRAVEL: = Body
*MOVE/LEAP: = Body -1
*MOVE/FLIGHT: 5 + Body + Agility
*MOVE/SWIMMING: 2 + Body + Strength

MEDIUM LIMITS
ENCUMBRANCE: Body + Strength
MOVE/COMBAT: 1 + Body + Agility
MOVE/TRAVEL: 1 + Body + Strength
*MOVE/LEAP: = Body -1
*MOVE/FLIGHT: 2 + Body + Agility
*MOVE/SWIMMING: Body + Strength

LARGE LIMITS
ENCUMBRANCE: 4 + Body + Strength
MOVE/COMBAT: Body + Agility
MOVE/TRAVEL: 2 + Body + Strength
*MOVE/LEAP: 0
*MOVE/FLIGHT: Body + Strength
*MOVE/SWIMMING: Body + Strength

*Only available to some species, not universal

GIANT LIMITS
ENCUMBRANCE: 10 + Body + Strength
MOVE/COMBAT: = Agility
MOVE/TRAVEL: 3 + Body + Strength
*MOVE/LEAP: 0
*MOVE/FLIGHT: = Body
*MOVE/SWIMMING: = Body

These Limits are average. Different species may have Limits that are higher or lower than the average. Only certain animals will have a Move/Leap or Move/Flight or Move/Swimming Limit, depending on species' abilities. All animals will have Encumbrance, even if it is 0. Only animals that are adapted to live life underwater 100% of the time, like most fish, will not have a Move/Combat or Move/Travel Limit.

DAMAGE	CLAW/HORN/HOOF	BITE/STOMP
Tiny	0	0
Small	1	1
Medium	2	2
Large	2	3
Giant	3	5

Animals with thick fur, feathers, or scales have a natural Padded armor defense.

Intelligent animals are able to have Mind and Spirit Scores as high as 3, and can learn and speak Languages. They will have 10, 20, or 30 points to spend on skills from the schools of Body, Mind, Spirit, Combat, and Strange. Some will have 5 points in one of the schools of Martial, Psionics, Divine, or Occult. Intelligent animals never learn skills from more than one school of Special/Magic Skills. Their Sanity and Morale Status levels are Attribute +2.

SIZE	ATTRIBUTE POINTS
Tiny	2
Small	3
Medium	6
Large	7
Giant	9

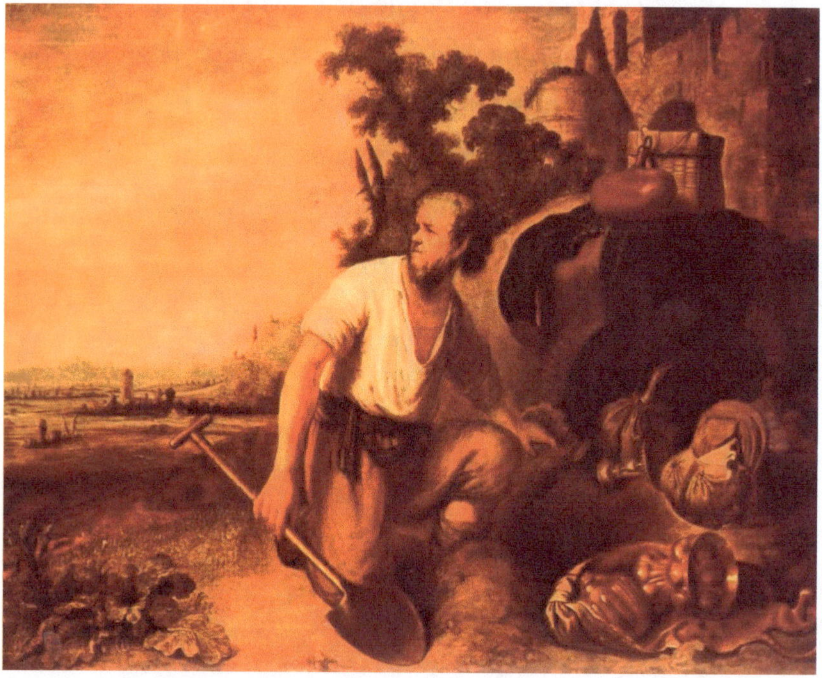

Fairy Treasure

Commerce and money were not quite as they are now, during the age of Fairy Tales. Sure, coins existed and people were paid and then taxed, and goods and services rendered. But modern concepts such stores to buy random products at fixed prices were not at all commonplace. The sort of thing one may see in the largest of towns, and cities. Most people worked from home, and traded from home. Commoners seldom saw the fancier coins of the Clergy or Nobility. You could not simply walk into any old village corner-store and plop $4.99 down on the counter and demand a box of arrows. Many goods had to be made after paying for their commission, and would have to be picked up when ready, or arrangements made for delivery.

And yet, money still existed, and was very important. Greed existed too. Greed by the barrel full. Many are the Fairy Tales where at some point our protagonists are at the very least tempted by great treasure, and many more will end with their heroes being richly rewarded for avoiding temptation in their earlier exploits.

But this is a role-playing game, not some simple bedtime story. Coins and bank loans aren't as fun for the Players as they may be for poor Peasant Characters, past the point of collection. The best Treasures they could find are the ones they will make use of, and nothing begs for Players to use them quite like Magic Items.

In the Rules Handbook, in the sections about Magic, guidelines are given for the creation of a variety of minor enchanted items. Objects which have been Blessed, Healing Potions, Candles containing Demonology spells, and Potions of Metamorphosis are all described, but items such as these pale in comparison to a true Magic Item.

One which has its own spirit and mind.

A "true" Magic Item is one which was crafted with both Science and Demonology to bind a spirit, willingly or unwillingly, into an object to imbue it with supernatural power. The spirits become one with the object they are bound to, keeping it resistant to breakage and decay, and able to sense what transpires around it, and whom it is currently being used by. Magic Items do not have Attributes or Skills as we known them, but they can telepathically view the thoughts and feelings, and through clairvoyance sense the future and past of, the people who handle them.

If the spirit in the Item takes a liking to someone, it will subtly plant thoughts into their mind to let them know what the item may be capable of doing, and how to make it do so. Magic Items are typically jealous and territorial beings, and will only let themselves be used by one person at a time, and only with people who are not bonded with any other true Magic Item.

Each Magic Item type has its own rules and conditions. A Magic Item can be disenchanted if it is the subject of an Exorcism ritual. A Magic Item must be disenchanted before it can be destroyed.

The following Magic Items are detailed in this Handbook:

MAGIC ITEMS	PAGE
Magic Weapon	283
Demon Arrow	285
Divine Shield	289
Wizard Staff	291
Fairy Wand	294
Magic Ring	298
Flying Broom	300
Magic Mirror	302
Crystal Ball	304
Magic Bag	305
Witch Cauldron	311
Invisible Clothing	314
Magic Boots	316
Hypnotic Instrument	318
Weatherproof Cloak	319
Magic Key	319
Dragonscale Armor	320
Magic Amulet	321

MAGIC WEAPONS

Magic Weapons include any Melee weapon such as Swords, Daggers, Axes, Spears, Clubs, Whips, or Hammers. They will have 1 of the following powers:

PYROKINESIS: The weapon's blade or head is engulfed with magically fueled fire that burns for as long as the weapon is bonded with its wielder. This increases the damage by +2, and the flames will cause combustible materials to catch fire if they make contact with the weapon for 2 consecutive turns. Flaming weapons cannot be doused. They will slowly burn and melt their scabbards, and wrapping them in wet cloth will only temporarily quench the fire. Within 5 minutes the heat will evaporate the moisture out of the towels or rags being used, and they will burst into flames. The only way to safely store a flaming weapon is to keep it submerged in water, or set on a stone or concrete surface out of reach of anything flammable.

CRYOKINESIS: The weapon constantly emits a freezing temperature along its surface, which causes moisture in the air to build up a sheath of ice. Frost Weapons increase their damage by +1, and the weapon can freeze water it is placed in at rate of a gallon per turn, and can freeze up to 100 gallons. A Frost Weapon can be sheathed if it is a blade, but it continues to emanate coldness, building up a layer of ice between the blade and its sheath. Unsheathing a Frost Blade thus requires an Average difficulty Strength action in order to ready the weapon.

PHOTOKINESIS: The weapon emits a constant noticeable glow that casts as much light as a torch when unsheathed in a darkened environment. The striking part of the weapon is also hot to the touch, though not as much as the Flaming Sword. A Light Weapon increases it damage by +1. The weapons glow can be diminished if the wielder is concentrating fully upon it, preventing them from being able to Move, talk, or take other actions while focusing on it.

TELEKINESIS: The weapon appears otherwise normal, but telekinetic force allows the wielder to throw it to make a ranged attack with a range of line-of-sight. The weapon will then spend the next turn flying back to its owner's hand. The added force from the telekinetic field increases the weapon's damage by +1. It also surrounds the user with a partial force field when being held, adding +4 to the wielder's Armor defense.

DEMON ARROWS

Demon Arrows are unique items, and must be manually retrieved in order to be reused. Even the most legendary of Archers has never had more than one Demon Arrow in their possession, as like any other magical item, they cannot share a telepathically linked owner with another Item's spirit. They have often been handed down as heirlooms along human bloodlines, and have been responsible for many assassinations, lucky shots in battle, and fallen wyverns over the centuries. They come in three varieties:

BLACK ARROWS:
Black Arrows can strike anything that is in the owner's line of sight and unobstructed. Distant targets that are moving will require that the shot be fired slightly off-target to intercept it when they reach the same point of collision (leading the target). The Black Arrow inflicts up to 10 points of Health damage to its target, and is instantly fatal to anything with 5 Health levels or less. The wielder will still have to make a successful Ranged attack

against the target's armor difficulty like a normal attack with a ranged weapon. The arrow requires a bow to be fired, it cannot be thrown, and only does 1 point of damage if used as an improvised stabbing melee weapon.

RED ARROWS:
If the tip of a Red Arrow is dipped in even the tiniest amount of blood, it will point towards the person where the blood came from when strung in a bow and held at-ready. If the target is in sight, the Arrow will be able to alter its trajectory mid-flight after it has been fired to maneuver around obstacles and score an automatic hit for 3 levels of Health damage, if the attack roll can beat the target's armor difficulty. Even diving into Full Cover will not deter the arrow as long as it is fired while the designated target is in sight. They are limited by the normal firing range of the Bow being used to fire them.

PURPLE ARROWS:

Purple Arrows are among the rarer types, as they are the only utility Arrow known to have been designed. Purple Arrows are made to carry massages to any target that the owner can clearly picture in their memory, for the Arrow to use to identify them. These arrows will always strike something nearby to the intended recipient of the note tied around it, and if anyone else fires this arrow from a bow once the message has been delivered, it will fly back to its owner. Otherwise, it must be retrieved or returned in-person.

DIVINE SHIELDS

Magic Shields were once more common, but most have been hidden away in the Church's archives. The few that are still in circulation are storied possessions.

HAND SHIELDS:

These shields provide a +2 bonus to Parry when equipped in the Character's off-hand, and when slung across the back do not count against their Encumbrance Limit like other Small Shields. When slung over the back in such a fashion, the owner can concentrate to turn invisible. They can make Move actions while doing so, but interacting with objects or making an attack will disrupt their concentration and they will become visible once more. Legends say the Gods made such shields for the greatest of mortal scouts and hunters in days of old.

BATTLE SHIELDS:

Battle Shields provide a +4 bonus to Parry and Dodge while equipped, and when slung across the back do not count against a Character's Encumbrance Limit, unlike normal Large Shields. They also make their owner immune to heat and flame while equipped or worn.

TOWER SHIELDS:

Magical Tower Shields count as an oversized Item when carried, but do not reduce Move Limits while carried. They provide a +6 bonus to Dodge and Parry, and extend this bonus to every other shield that is locked into the same Shield Wall as a Magic Tower Shield. Most of these relics hail from ancient Rome or Greece, and they are less useful in later periods than the other types of Magic Shields.

WIZARD STAFFS

Also known as Druid Staffs, the exact secret of their creation was lost two thousand years ago. Only three are known to remain, and it is believed that within them is the soul of an ancient and powerful wizard, whose mastery of magic made them as powerful as any other spirit used to craft magical weapons.

STONE-BREAKER:
Any object made from rock, stone, or concrete that is tapped with the base of this staff will crack in half. The owner must concentrate on the effect while actively stabbing their staff at the surface of the object they wish to break. In particularly huge structures, such as building exteriors or cliffs, this effect will shatter enough of the surface area that repeated use will punch a hole through the material large enough for two people to walk through side by side, with minimal headroom. The Staff also imparts a heavier impact when used to strike a living opponent, doing 3 levels of Health damage on a successful attack. The staff has no effect on

sand, mud, and other soft surfaces, nor on metal, wood, and other formerly living tissues.

STORM-MAKER:
This Staff generates a constant effect that causes cloudy weather and intermittent precipitation in a 25 mile radius of wherever the Staff is located while actively linked to an owner. This effect can be dispelled if the owner concentrates upon it, which will hold off the rain for a number of hours equal to the owner's Spirit+Focus, before the clouds start to gather again. The user can also concentrate while holding the staff to increase precipitation and storm conditions, which can take up to several hours depending on the severity of the desired weather. Weather created in this way will dissipate at a natural rate for the environment and time of year in the Storm-Maker's location. If the generated weather has at least reached severe thunderstorm levels of intensity, the Staff's owner can concentrate for 2 Turns to direct a bolt of lightning at a target in their line of sight, doing 5 levels of Health damage to everything within 10 feet of the target.

FIRE-BREATHER:

This Staff, when concentrated upon, will shoot a jet of flame from the head of the staff in a continuous line of flame that has a range equal to the wielder's Spirit Score. The flames do 2 levels of Health damage per turn of contact to anything that the line of flames touches, and will ignite flammable materials after 1 Turn. While in use, the user must maintain their concentration, and can only re-aim where the flame is projected, or make a Move action at half their normal Limit, rounding down. The Staff also has the side effect of making the owner immune to heat and fire while they are holding the Fire-Breather Staff.

Wizard Staffs are extremely potent weapons of magic, and most of them have been lost over the centuries due to the conflicts that erupt between those who covet possession of one of the Staffs for themselves. Despite their ancient origins, they have travelled around the world and back several times since their creation, and are known by different names in different legends in different lands.

FAIRY WANDS

Fairy Wands are very rare, and grow harder to find with each passing year. Fairy Wands look like your classic magic wand, made from delicate wood, finely crafted rare metals, or from huge solid gemstones carefully chiseled into shape. They come in four different types:

CHARMING WANDS:
When the owner points this type of Wand at a target in their Line of Sight and concentrates on the effect, the target will lose 1 level of Morale Status per Turn as their will is bent to serving the wielder of the wand. When first attacked, they may make a Hard Mind+Focus action to realize what is going on and move enough to break the wand's stream of energy towards them (visible with Shadow Sight). If they fail this roll, they will feel euphoric and not notice their Morale drain. Once they have become Incapacitated they will act as if in love with the Wand's owner and will do whatever they are told to do by them. If their Morale becomes critically damaged by the effect, they will

develop a telepathic link with their new master which allows them to know what is wanted of them before being told verbally.

TIME WANDS:
This Wand, when pointed at a target and concentrated upon, does damage to the target's Health Status, ignoring body armor and martial skills, by rapidly aging them. For each turn the wand is pointed at the target, they will lose 1 level of Health if they fail to succeed at a Body+Focus action. The target will feel the effect as extreme agony, and can use their turn to Move and disrupt the effect, if they are not bound in place.

BINDING WANDS:
Binding Wands, when pointed at a Ghost or other Spiritual entity (and occultists who are Astral Projecting), will hold them in place and make them visible to people in the Mortal World who would not otherwise be able to see into Astral Space. The entity will remain immobilized for as long as the Wand's owner keeps it pointed at the spirit, and concentrates on the effect. The captured entity will

only be able to speak, if it is capable of such things, until it is released. The Wand can also allow the owner to see into Astral Space by holding it in front of them and concentrating as they look around.

PORTAL WANDS:
These powerful but dangerous Wands can open a door in space-time allowing the owner of the wand and a number of companions equal to the owner's Spirit Score to pass through and teleport to the last location the Wand was used at. The roughly human-sized portal will open wherever the owner points the wand when they concentrate on opening it, which takes 2 full Turns without interruption.

Once on the other side of the gateway, further use of the Wand will open a portal to wherever the Wand had been used previously to the last time it had been used at that location, and so on, allowing the user to potentially teleport all the way back to wherever the Wand had been created. A dangerous path, as over the centuries many of the locations recorded by a Portal Wand will have become uninhabitable or deadly in some form or fashion. Buried under rock, flooded, filled with radiation, now in the middle of a shopping mall, the potential horrors are endless for those who travel back too far along their Wand's recorded history.

The Wand must travel at least 5 miles away from a point it has recorded in order to not teleport any further down the Wand's recorded history, in order to return to the original recorded location they began their current teleportation sequence at.

Opening a portal on or in a living being is immediately fatal to them.

MAGIC RINGS

Magic Rings have always been a popular Magic Item for the Religious and Nobility. They must be worn for their powers to become active, and removed for their effect to end. Some of those still to be found out there include:

RINGS OF DISGUISE
A Ring of Disguise uses a subtle psychic effect to make anyone who does not know the person wearing it to see whomever they would expect to see in their location and/or circumstance, that is most non-suspicious to them. Anyone who already knows the wearer of this ring will see them as they really are. The effect is purely in the mind of those looking at the ring's wearer, it does not actually change their appearance physically, or create an illusion that other people could see. This ring effects anything with sentient intelligence, including Ghosts and Spirits. Powers and spells that allow someone to see a target's true form or identity will be able to see through the ring's suggestive effect.

RING OF SWORDS

Anytime the wearer of this ring wants to be holding a sword, and they are not already holding a weapon, a sword will appear in the hand that the ring is being worn on. It is a normal sword that does 2 damage and is real for as long as the wearer of the ring holds it. If they let go of the sword it immediately vanishes.

DEFLECTION RING

The wearer of this ring gains a +4 bonus to Dodge and Parry. They will be unable to pick up, use, or hold any item until the ring is removed.

PILOT RING

The wearer of this ring gains the ability to fly telekinetically, with a top speed of 50 miles per hour, and a maximum altitude of 1,000 feet above solid and liquid surfaces beneath them. The wearer gains a Move/Flight Limit. If the wearer is already able to fly naturally, this ring doubles their Move/Flight Limit while worn.

RING MOVE/FLIGHT: 5 + Spirit + Focus

RING OF FISHES

This ring imparts the simple power to breathe underwater, and tolerate depth pressures of up to 1/4 mile below sea-level. Non-aquatic wearers will still be limited to a swimming speed of half their Move/Travel Limit (rounded down).

MAGIC BROOM

These items are coveted by Witches, and are telekinetically animated sentient brooms, which can carry their owner/rider and up to 1 human-sized passenger as they telekinetically fly through the air. They can also bash someone with their handle if they are not being ridden, as well as do light sweeping chores around the home. The rider must concentrate on directing the broom's flight, but if they have a passenger, they may use their Turn to perform any action they could conceivably do while trying to hold onto a flying broom between their legs, which admittedly isn't much.

The broom can hover in place, or accelerate up to a speed of 200 miles per hour. Passengers must succeed at an Average Body+Strength action to not fall off during high-speed (over 50 mph) maneuvers. Its Bash Attack does 1 damage to Health, and the broom rolls its attack with 1D6 and a +5 bonus. The broom cannot fly with extra cargo, just their passengers and their passengers own carried items.

The Broom can respond to verbal and telepathic commands, and will fly to their owner's location if summoned. Flying Brooms have the following Limit value:

MOVE/FLIGHT: 10

The one major drawback to owning a Flying Broom is that they only function at night, after sunset and until the moment of sunrise.

MAGIC MIRRORS

Magic Mirrors will offer one of three abilities when their owner looks into them and concentrates on someone they want to see. If the person in question happens to be within line-of-sight of another mirror, or a reflective surface like still water, the mirror will show a version of the target that the Magic Mirror's owner can interact with. What they can do depends on which kind of mirror it is:

PSYCHIC MIRROR
This mirror will show an avatar of the owner's target, which they can talk with and try to charm or interrogate them long enough to get 1 secret of out them. After a secret has been revealed, the mirror cannot be used again until the next sunrise. The target will have no memory of this occurring.

DIVINE MIRROR
This mirror will display the owner's target in their true form; if they have been using magic, disguise, or deceit to obscure their real identity.

WITCH MIRROR

This mirror does not reveal a distant target. Instead it will show any Ghost or spirit that exists in Astral Space within its field of view.

Magic Mirrors come in a variety of sizes: Tall standing mirrors, wall mounted mirrors, table mirrors, hand held mirrors, and pocket mirrors.

Magic Mirrors cannot be broken or destroyed unless disenchanted first with Exorcism. The mirror's owner, however, can smash and crack the mirror's surface, but it will magically repair itself the next time its owner isn't paying attention to it.

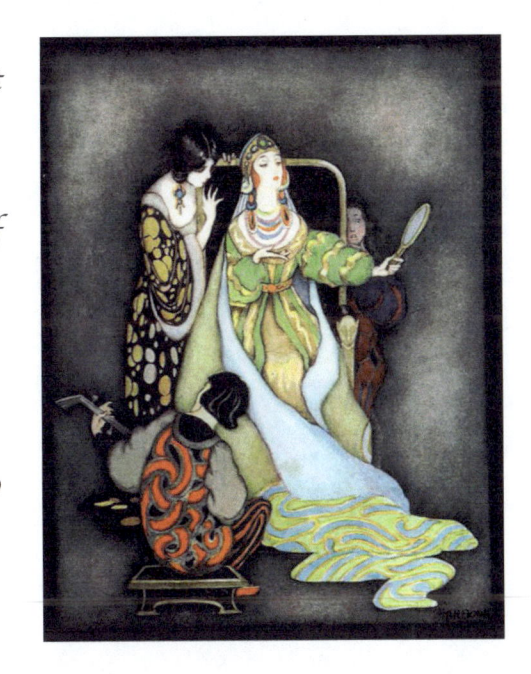

CRYSTAL BALLS

Crystal Balls are small orbs of fine crystal that can be held in the palm of a hand, and are somewhere between the size of a baseball and a basketball for reference.

A Crystal Ball is tuned to one of the three Psionics Skills: Clairvoyance (Seer's Ball), Psychokinesis (Sorcerer's Ball), or Telepathy (Scanner's Ball). When the owner is within 10 feet (1 space) of their Crystal Ball, and it is uncovered and within their field of vision (they do not have to be looking directly at it but they must be capable of seeing it if only peripherally), the orb will grant a bonus of +3 to the Psionics skill the Ball is tuned to. This can either boost the owner's existing Psionics skill when used, or it will grant a non-psychic owner the ability to use that Psionics skill and its powers.

Non-psychics can use it to justify adding points to that Psionics skill when they gain levels of experience that grant skill points.

If the Crystal Ball is more than 10 feet away from its owner, but they can see it, their owner can concentrate for a Turn to make the Ball telekinetically fly to their hand, if it is not covered or otherwise secured in place.

MAGIC BAGS

Magic Bags come in several varieties, and all share the feature that if they are ever lost or stolen, they will magically teleport themselves back to their owners somewhere between 24 and 48 hours after they were first noticed to have gone missing. Anything placed inside them while they were away from their owner will still be inside them when they are later found somewhere in the owner's close vicinity.

Magic Bags are not easy to destroy. They have a durability of 20, and can be repaired if they reach Durability 0, unless the damage was from fire, which can destroy the bag. If a Magic Bag is destroyed, anything held within it with its magic is either lost, killed, or likewise destroyed.

COMMAND BAG

Any non-sentient animal or monster up to the size of a horse, or sentient mortal or supernatural creature that can understand the language of the Bag's Owner, will be magically compelled to go into the bag and enter a form of dreamless stasis if the Owner commands them to do so. The bag will magically enlarge to accommodate anything larger than its normal size (big enough for a turkey or goose). Once its occupant is inside, the bag returns to its normal size and appears empty. They can be removed if the owner commands them to come out, or if the owner dies. Only one creature at a time can be held in the Command Bag in this manner. When not being used to mystically contain someone or something, it can be used as a normal carrying sack, adding +2 to the owner's Encumbrance as long as they are not holding anything else in their hands. It must be emptied before it can be used to command someone to get inside of it.

DEVOURING BAG

Anything that can be placed into this bag, which has an opening roughly 2 and 1/2 feet across, and is 3 feet deep, will disappear and never return five minutes after the bag is closed. Even the owner cannot bring back anything lost in the bag. It is gone forever, from all levels of existence.

MONEY BAG

Money Bags appear as tiny coin-purses, and once per day the Owner can open it to find just enough coins to make a small to average purchase, depending on the local currencies. The money is always in a regionally appropriate coin format, and gives no indication that it is counterfeit in any way. Money placed into it by its owner can be retrieved later with a few extra coins of the same type added if they wait a day or more. Anyone else trying to get into the Money bag will find it empty, even if the money in it was real and placed there by its owner.

ACTION BAG

Action Bags look like empty sacks about 2 and a 1/2 feet wide at the opening, and 3 feet deep. They always appear empty, but the Owner can store any object that can fit through the bag's opening, and have it not count against their carrying Encumbrance Limit. The bag can be folded up and stuffed in a pocket, leaving their hands free for weapons or other items, and anyone inspecting the bag will think it is empty and worthless. Owners of this Bag can use it to smuggle all manner of contraband, and it can hold up to 20 Items in total. To retrieve an Item, their owner must concentrate on the object they want before opening the bag to reach in and pull it out. This bag only works on non-living non-magical objects. It cannot hide other Magical Items, Blessed objects, or enchanted objects, and the bag will not work until these items are removed from its interior. Items left in the bag by anyone other than the owner will remain in the bag as if it were a normal mundane sack, unless the Owner takes it out, and then deliberately puts it back into the bag.

Small, pocket sized items that wouldn't count against Encumbrance unless carried in a large quantity still count as single items when placed in the Action Bag, coins and money included, although an item containing other items, like a first aid kit or tool box, or a small chest of coins, can be placed in the bag as a single object, as long as it doesn't contain anything living or magical.

TOOL BAG

This old fashioned canvas tool-bag can hold up to +3 Encumbrance in small Items, plus when the Owner concentrates for a Turn and reaches in, they will pull out any small to medium sized tool they may need for any construction, carpentry, mechanical, technological, or even emergency and medical utility. It will not produce weapons or ammunition, but can provide tools needed for their construction, modification, or upkeep. Hammers, saws, and some bladed tools can be used as melee weapons in a pinch, but they will break after two uses, and do the minimal amount of damage as they can for their type. They can not pull out another tool they had not placed in the Bag themselves until the last magic one they used is returned. Returned tools disappear until summoned again. Tools created by this bag gives whomever uses them a +3 to any repair or recovery actions made while using them.

RAT BAG
This cursed item is said to have belonged to the Pied Piper of Hamlin, who used it to create the infestation he then "saved" the town from, before stealing all the townsfolk's children. The Rat bag appears as a dirty sack of the usual size. When open and held upside down, the bag can be shaken to release a number of rats that will come tumbling out to the ground, equal in number to the Owner's Spirit+Empathy, once per Turn as an action. Any normal object placed into the bag will have a rat clinging to it when the Owner retrieves it. If someone other than the owner opens the bag a single rat will jump out at them and scurry away, and they will have to make a Hard Mind+Focus roll or take 1 level of damage to their Sanity. The sack adds +2 to Encumbrance.

These rats are normal rats that will scurry away and hide if they can, once released. They do not understand nor obey the commands of the bag's owner, but someone with the right spells or psionics could conceivably control them.

WITCH CAULDRONS

Witch Cauldrons are over-sized items when carried empty, and too heavy for one person to move enough to qualify as a Move action when the cauldron has liquid in it. Witch Cauldrons are large cast-iron cooking pots that have been infused with a spirit to enhance one of their owner's Occult skills when they use it to cast spells. The Cauldron must be set over a fire with a stew or some other concoction set to a boil inside of it. With the addition of a special ingredient, a spell of the correct Occult skill that is then cast while stirring the Cauldron's contents has a +3 bonus to its casting roll, and any range or duration the spell has will be doubled. Unlike the Crystal Ball, only owners who already know the appropriate Occult skill for their type of Cauldron may use it.

Demon Cauldrons enhance Demonology, and require the addition of crystals ground into dust. A large quantity of salt does qualify, but must be busted up from the same block of salt. Sea salt will not work, it must be mined or from a lick. If someone ingests the contents of this Cauldron after a spell has been cast through it, they will be Easy for Demons, Fairies, and other spirits to possess until sunrise. The Cauldron can brew enough contents for 10 doses of this liquid.

Potion Cauldrons enhance Metamorphosis, and can be used to make "normal" Metamorphosis potions with a +3 bonus to the owner's spell casting to enchant the potion. A Cauldron can brew enough to make 10 potions at a time, but will have to be cooled down and cleaned out before it can make another batch. An average batch takes 12 hours to make. They will require at least 1 Health level's worth of human blood stirred into the mixture before the owner casts their spell into the brew to activate the potions' magic.

Death Cauldrons enhance Necromancy, and require the sacrifice of a Tiny sized animal (non-insect) such as a mouse, lizard, frog, or songbird, added live to the boiling brew before casting a spell through the Cauldron. If the contents of this Cauldron are ingested after a Necromancy spell has been cast through it the drinker will instantly die, if Mortal, with no chance for Shrugging damage, Strength actions to resist, or medical recovery to resuscitate them. On Fairies, Nymphs, and Cherubs, the Cauldron poison will Incapacitate them and trigger their teleportation to their place of recovery. On Shapeshifters other than Nymphs, ingesting the poison will make them transform into their animal form permanently, but will keep their sentient mind intact. This Cauldron can brew enough to produce 10 doses of this Magic Poison. It can be used to coat certain weapons like other poisons, or can be mixed into food or drink if not ingested directly from the Cauldron. It takes 24 hours to brew a batch of Magic Poison, and the Cauldron will need to be emptied and cleaned before it can be used to make any more.

INVISIBLE CLOTHING

There is only one set of Invisible Clothes in the world, and each garment is a separate Magic Item. They were commissioned many centuries ago by an Emperor who found he could not wear them all at once. They have since been separated and scattered to the corners of the world. When not being worn, they look like high quality garments of the sort a high-ranking Nobleman would wear during the previous era. They all grant the same abilities to their current owner when they are worn:

Invisibility.

The wearer is only visible to themselves. Even Ghosts and spirits cannot see them. Only powers that specifically grant "true sight" or "reveal true forms" will work to reveal someone wearing one of these garments. They make stealth actions at Easy difficulty unless in extremely small spaces with multiple people. They do make noise, and can be detected at Hard difficulty if the wearer is not trying to be stealthy. Invisible Characters are

Impossible difficulty to hit with an attack. Objects picked up by an Invisible Character become invisible too unless they are oversized, or would exceed the Character's Encumbrance Limit.

The following Invisible Garments were Created. Only one of each (with a slight exception for the paired items) exists:

Invisible Hat
Invisible Coat
Invisible Vest
Invisible Shirt
Invisible Belt
Invisible Pants
Invisible Cape
*Invisible Gloves (pair)
*Invisible Socks (pair)

*Both must be worn for the Invisibility to take effect.

Any items carried or worn by the Character wearing an invisible garment are also invisible.

MAGIC BOOTS

Magic Boots are typically old but sturdy-looking work boots made for Commoners. They come in pairs, and both must be worn for their powers to take effect on their wearer. There are four common types of Magic Boots:

SKIPPING BOOTS
These Magic Boots give their wearer an incredible Move/Leap Limit:

MOVE/LEAP: 1 + Spirit + Agility

WALKING BOOTS
These Magic Boots allow their wearers to walk incredible distances before they must rest, giving them the following Limit value when worn:

MOVE/TRAVEL: 10 + Body + Focus

The wearer of these Boots will use their normal Move/Travel Limit to determine Move rates while swimming (1/2 speed rounded down), not the Limit granted by the boots.

STOMPING BOOTS

Stomping Boots give their wearer a +2 bonus to both Dodge and Parry while worn, and can be used to make a Kick attack that inflicts a number of levels of Health damage equal to their wearer's Body Score +1.

CLIMBING BOOTS

These boots alter the pull of gravity for whoever wears them, allowing them to walk up steep to vertical surfaces at a comfortable walking speed. The boots will slip if the surface is tilted at an angle facing the ground, or is upside down. When walking sideways up a surface the wearer must keep at least one foot on the surface they are walking on at all times. Jumping or attempting to run will cause the boots to slip, and the wearer to fall and potentially take damage (1 Health level per 10 feet fallen, damage can be Shrugged off). Most climbing actions will automatically succeed, or their difficulties will be greatly reduced (Average difficulty at most), when wearing these boots.

HYPNOTIC INSTRUMENTS

Hypnotic Instruments are Musical items like pipes, flutes, lutes, harps, guitars, trumpets, fiddles, accordions, and other hand-held musical instruments that make tonal sounds of some sort or another. Drums and cymbals can not be made as Hypnotic Instruments. When used to perform a song (Mind+Art or Spirit+Technology, Hard difficulty), those who can hear the music will be Easy to manipulate afterwards with Charisma and Telepathy actions for a duration equal to the duration of the song performed. If the song was interrupted or halted prematurely, the magic does not take effect on the audience. Those whom are manipulated during this period must succeed at a Very difficult Mind+Focus action to realize they've been tricked later on. The difficulty is Hard if they've been manipulated to do something against their interests or usual behavioral norms. A proper song must be performed, not a random or idle tune. Other musicians with instruments and/or lyrical accompaniment are optional. Fellow performers are not effected by the instrument's magic.

WEATHERPROOF CLOAK

A Weatherproof Cloak is a simple but handy Magical Item that looks like a quality-made cloak with a hood, and fur lining. When worn, the cloak's owner will be completely unaffected by the weather. Rain, Snow, Extreme Cold, Wind, and Heat, both humid and dry, will not effect the wearer while the hood is pulled up over their head. When they take off their cloak, they will be dry and clean and neither hair nor clothes will be ruffled. The user is effectively immune to cold and heat based damage as well, but direct contact with flame will still burn both cloak and wearer.

MAGIC KEY

This Golden Key will fit any lock and open it. Once used it will turn to Iron and fall out of the keyhole. It will be unusable on any lock until the next sunrise, when it will turn Golden again until used once more. These keys are Easy for their owner to conceal in their palm or clothing.

DRAGONSCALE ARMOR

Dragonscale Armor is a Full Suit of Knight Plate armor, which has been stylistically crafted to evoke dragon scales and features. Most of the armor is made of manufactured materials, but it will incorporate some small amount of materials from an actual dragon: patches of skin turned to leather, horns and scales, teeth, or claws can all be used to create this armor. It provides Impossible difficulty armor defense, makes their wearer immune to fire and heat based attacks, and gives them a +2 Bonus to both Strength and Charisma. It also gives them a Leaping Limit while worn:

MOVE/LEAP: = Body

If worn with the Helmet removed, it still gives the wearer Full Suit protection (Very difficult), and its other abilities remain active.

MAGIC AMULETS

When worn, a Magic Amulet surrounds its owner with a Force Field, making them Impossible difficulty to attack. The Amulet itself decides what it will prevent the wearer from making contact with, and will block all incoming attacks. If the Amulet's spirit senses danger in an object or a person, it may prevent its wearer from being able to touch or hold them. The Amulet must be worn around the neck as a piece of jewelry, which will grant the usual +1 Bonus to Beauty if it is not concealed under clothing or armor. The wearer is always able to touch and remove the Amulet, preventing angry or vindictive spirits from potentially abusing their owner. The Force Field is invisible unless struck, which will cause a brief shimmer of energy at the point of contact.

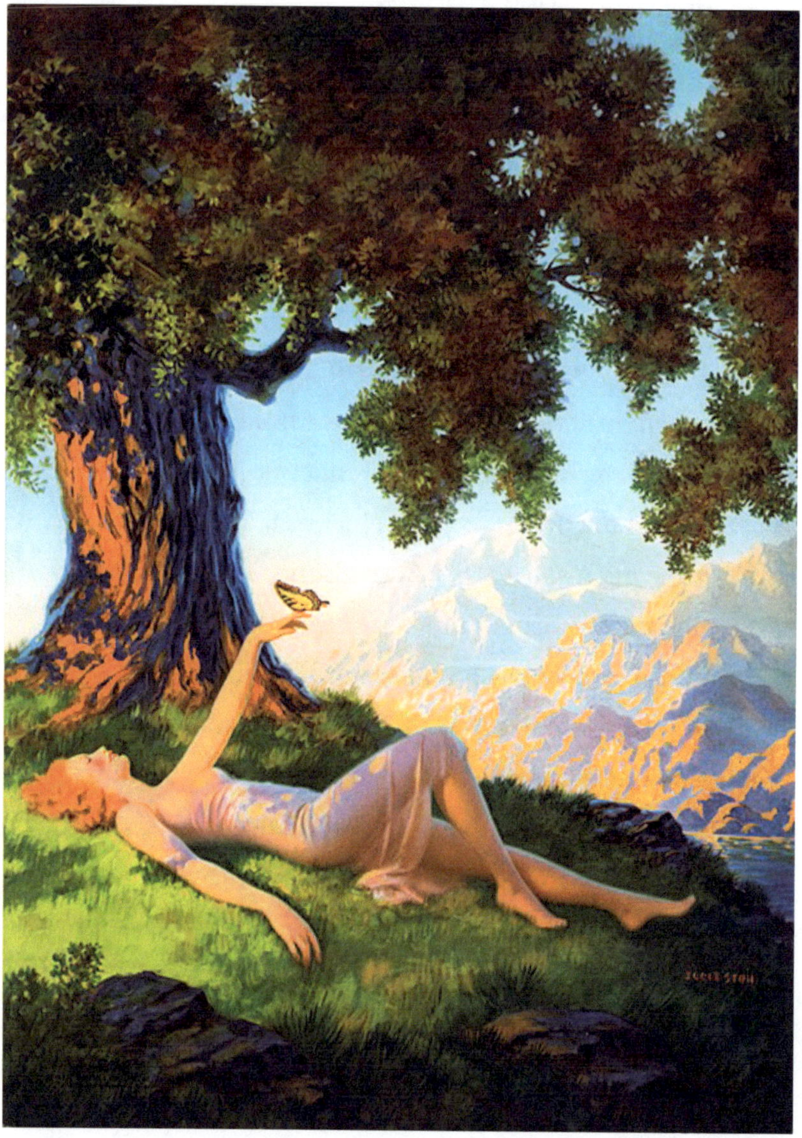

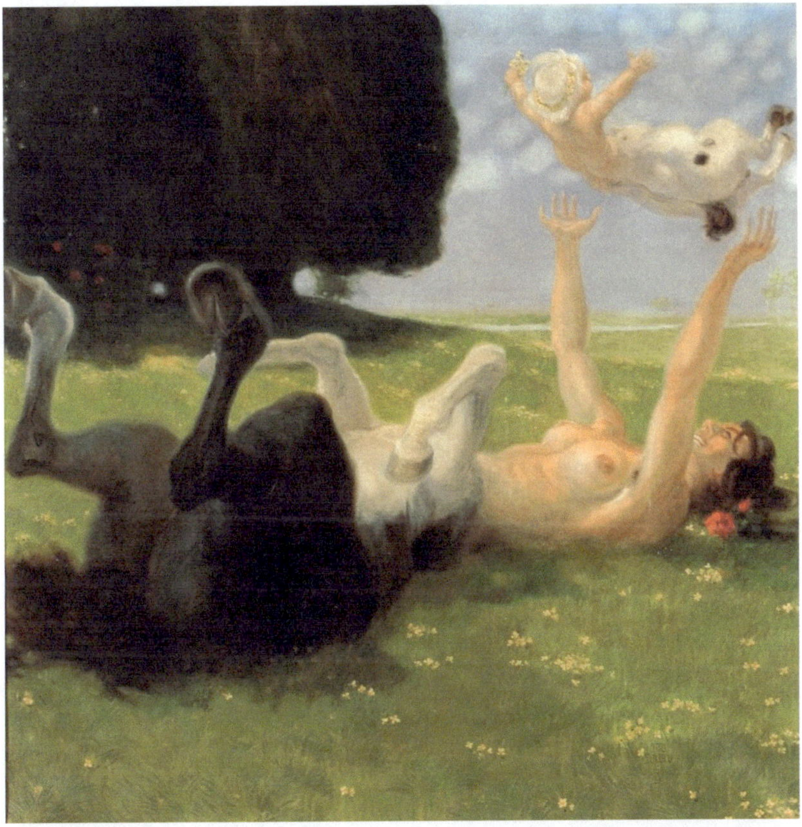

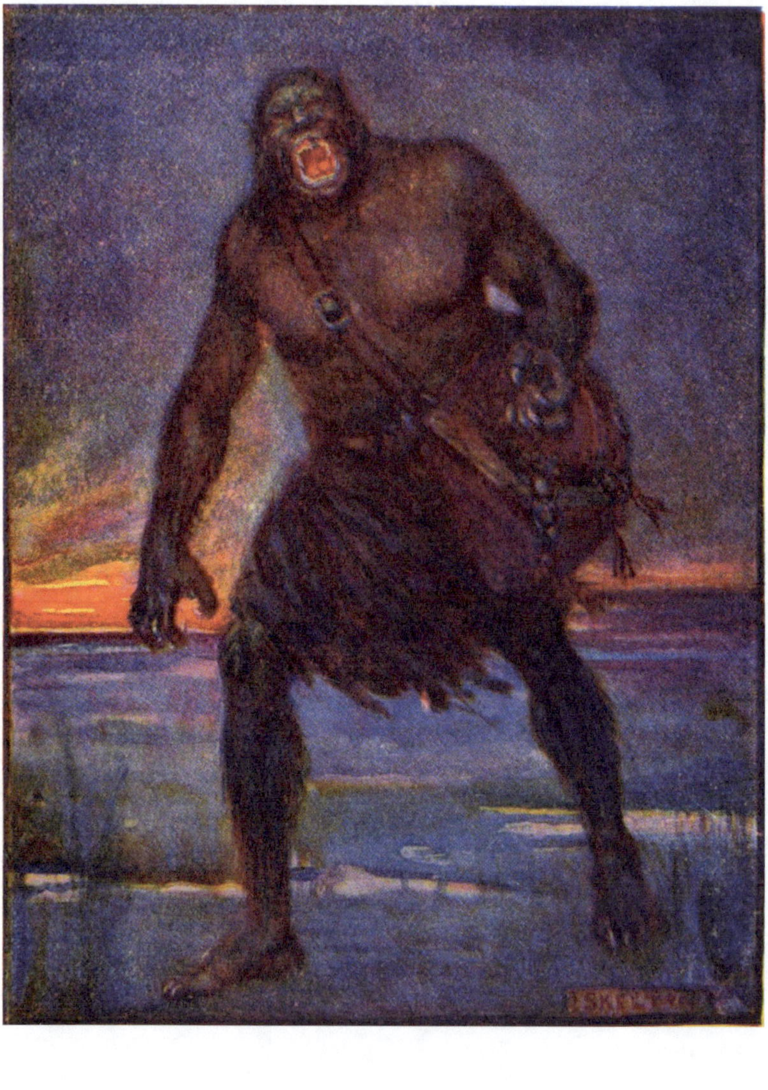

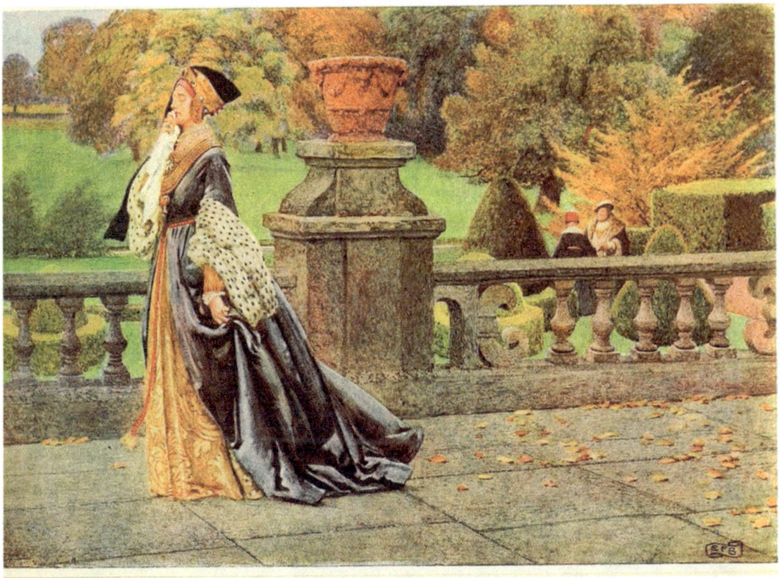

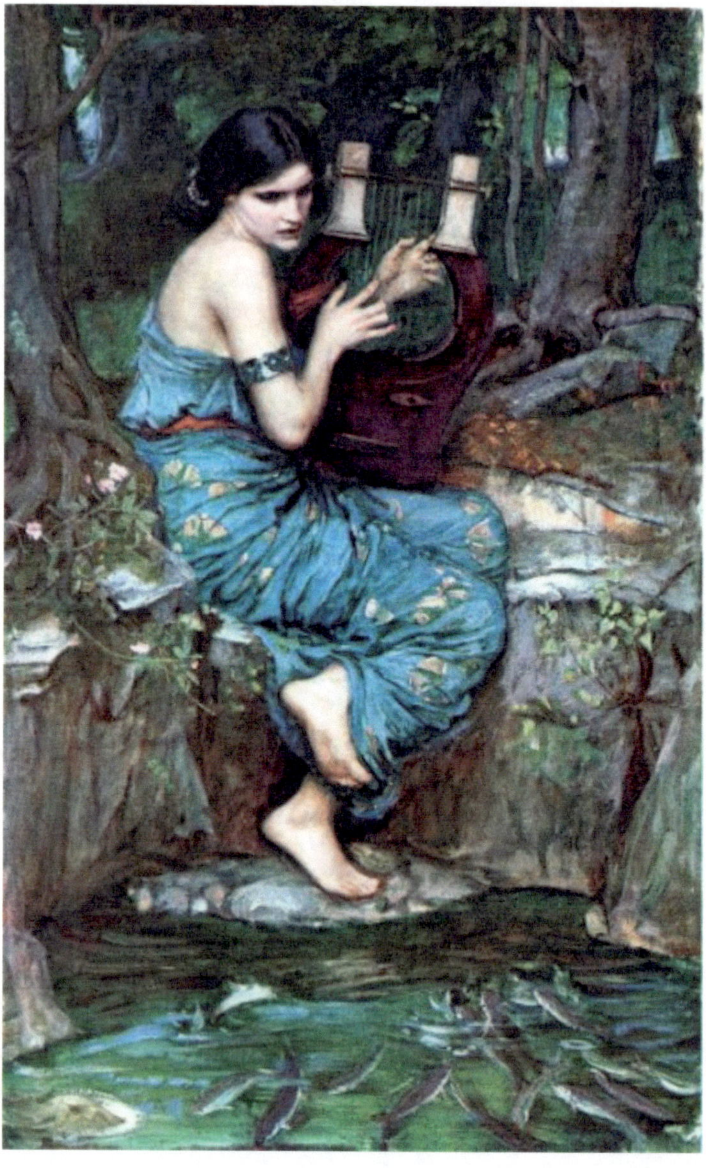

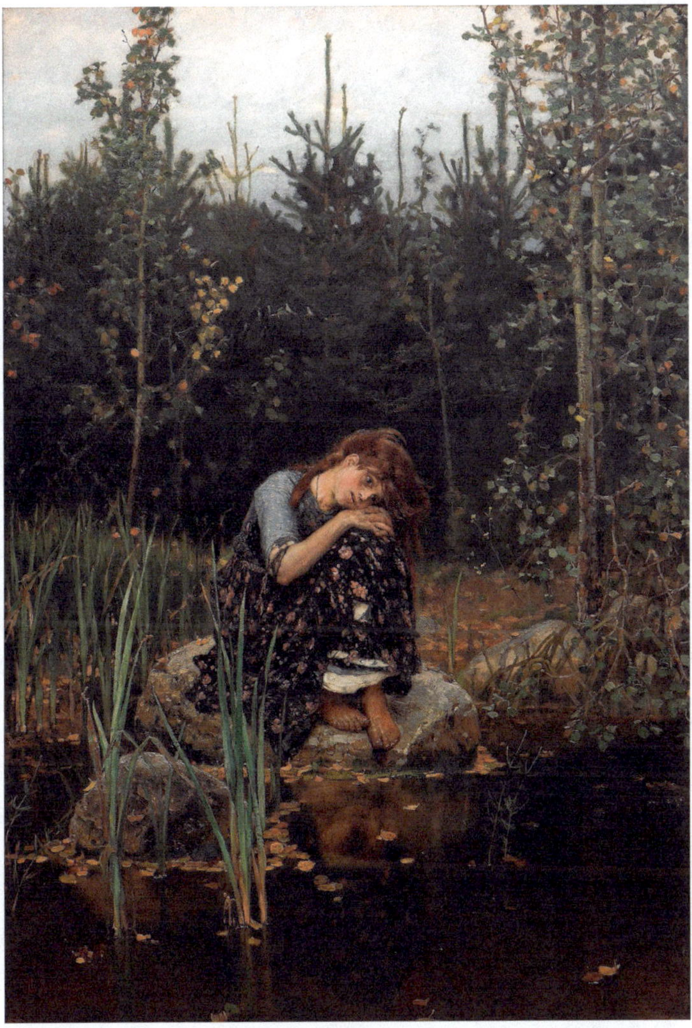

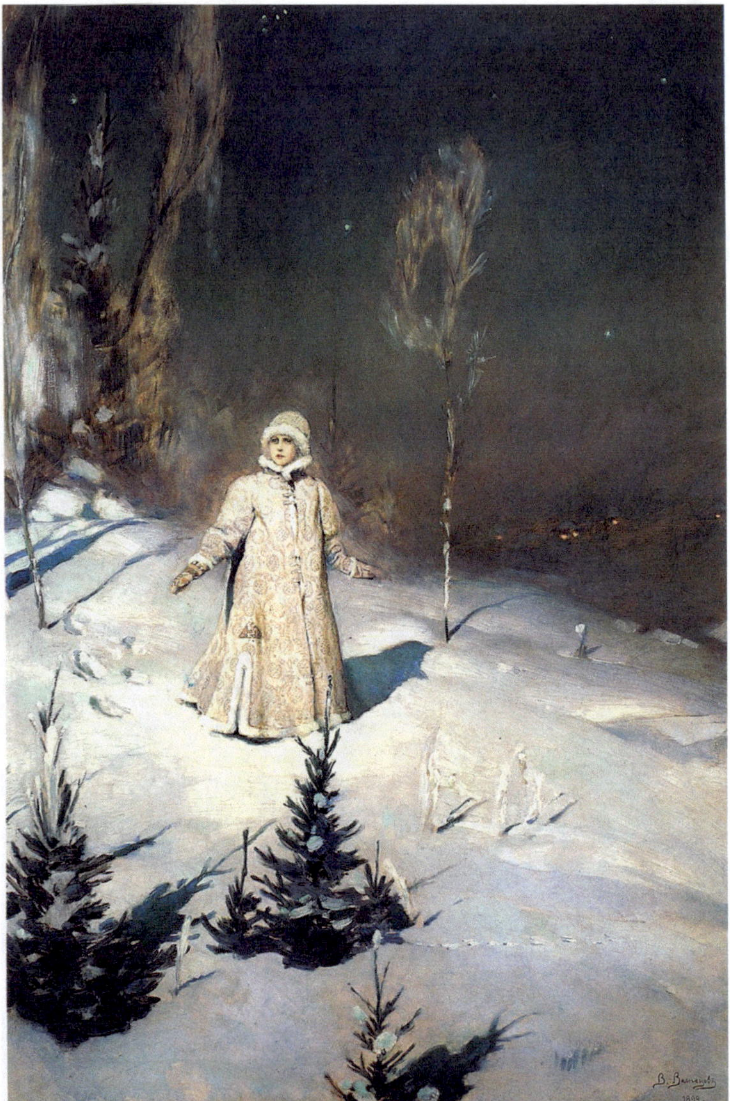

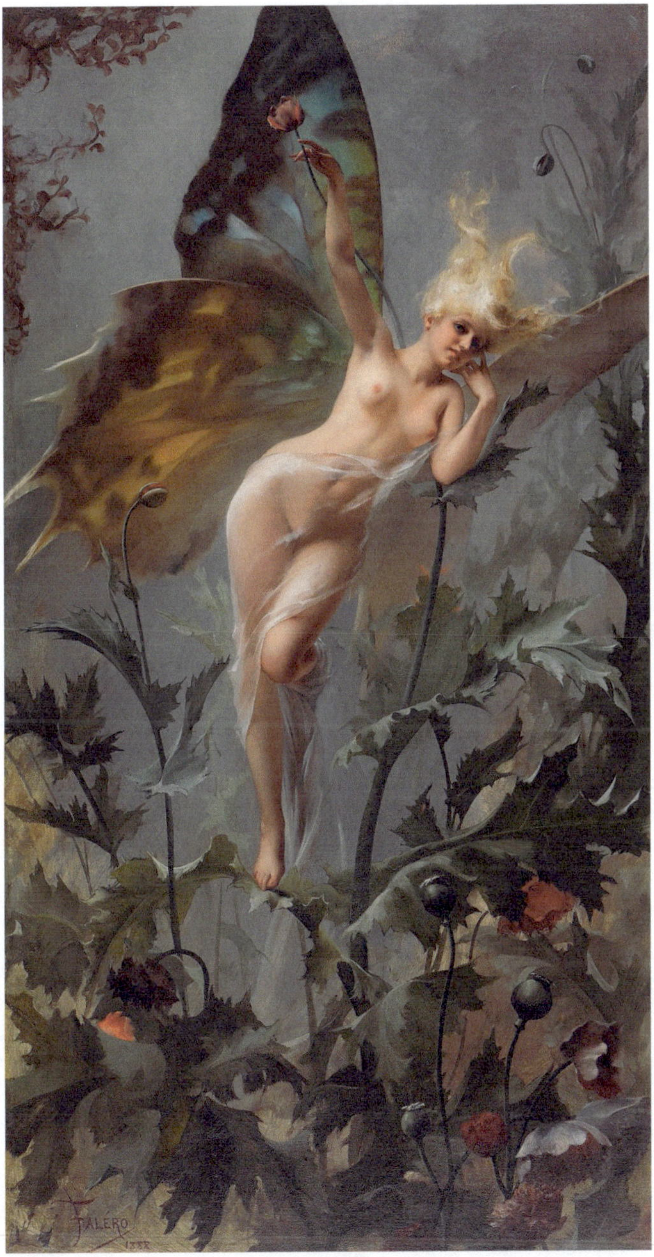
FALERO

Available Now:

the TOTAL PARTY SYSTEM
RULES HANDBOOK
Setting-Agnostic Universal RPG! by Total Party Skills

"The Total Party System Fairy Tale Handbook"
By Total Party Skills
Copyright 2024 R Joshua Holland

Made in the USA
Columbia, SC
04 February 2024